Women Lovers, or The Third Woman

Natalie Clifford Barney

Edited and translated by Chelsea Ray

THE UNIVERSITY OF WISCONSIN PRESS

The University of Wisconsin Press
1930 Monroe Street, 3rd Floor
Madison, Wisconsin 53711-2059
uwpress.wisc.edu

3 Henrietta Street, Covent Garden
London WC2E 8U, United Kingdom
eurospanbookstore.com

First published in France as *Amants féminins, ou, La troisième,*
copyright © 2013 ErosOnyx Éditions
Translation copyright © 2016 The Board of Regents of the
University of Wisconsin System

Printed in the United States of America
This book may be available in a digital edition.

Library of Congress Cataloging-in-Publication Data
Names: Barney, Natalie Clifford, author. | Ray, Chelsea, 1972–
editor, translator.
Title: Women lovers, or The third woman / Natalie Clifford Barney ;
edited and translated by Chelsea Ray.
Other titles: Amants féminins, ou, La troisième. English
Description: Madison, Wisconsin : The University of Wisconsin Press, [2016] |
© 2016 | First published in France as Amants féminins, ou, La troisième,
© 2013 ErosOnyx. | Includes bibliographical references.
Identifiers: LCCN 2015041317 | ISBN 9780299306908 (cloth : alk. paper)
Subjects: LCSH: Lesbians—France—Paris—Fiction.
Classification: LCC PQ3939.B3 A813 2016 | DDC 843/.912—dc23
LC record available at http://lccn.loc.gov/2015041317

Women Lovers, or
The Third Woman

Publication of this volume has been made possible, in part, through support from the Brittingham Fund.

To
MICHAEL HEIM,
whose passion for translation is contagious

To
MY PARENTS,
who sent me to France in the first place

and

To
GREG,
for "all that there is"

Contents

Acknowledgments

From the time I read this manuscript in the archives of the Bibliothèque Littéraire Jacques Doucet until its publication, there have been many people along the way who offered help, advice, and support. I would like to thank François Chapon, literary executor of the Natalie Clifford Barney estate, for granting me permission to publish this work. In addition, I wish to thank the staff at the Bibliothèque for affording me so much help during my year of research. I am grateful for Yvan Quintin's support in publishing the novel in French with ErosOnyx Éditions. I am also thankful for my conversations with Jean Chalon, Francesco Rapazzini, and Suzanne Rodrigue, who helped to bring Barney's world to life for me. I am grateful to Emily Apter, who supported my work on Barney in innumerable ways.

I would like to thank the University of Wisconsin Press for its support in this project, especially Raphael Kadushin and Adam Mehring.

I have also received extraordinary assistance in the translation process. Melanie Hawthorne supported the project from the beginning and provided extensive editorial notes; Jean-Claude Redonnet spent countless hours with me at his kitchen table mulling over passages; Suzanne Stroh and Jean-Loup Combemale gave expert editing and translation advice; Claire Soulié provided detailed feedback on specific translation challenges; and Michael Heim sparked my love of translation in his workshops at UCLA and later worked on key passages with me in his garden in Los Angeles. Many others have given me a hand, including my French "uncle," Jean Ruaud, and my French host "parents," Solange and Patrick Nérission. Their teaching and kindness helped me to grasp the French language as a teenager and continue to this day.

It is impossible to name all the other writers and scholars whose work helped me along the path. Michèle Causse's work on the *souvenirs* of Berthe Cleyrergue introduced me to Barney for the very first time; Karla Jay's literary study of Barney and Renée Vivien was groundbreaking; Shari Benstock's work opened up this world in Paris to me; Cassandra Langer served as inspiration for the completion of this project and illuminated Barney's life for me; Jean Chalon's and George Wickes's biographies were essential; Joan DeJean's work helped me to better understand the context; Bridget Elliot and Jo-Ann Wallace showcased women and modernism; Tama Lea Engelking foregrounded Barney's relationship to Delarue-Mardrus and was thoroughly supportive; Anna Livia's important translations were inspiring; Diana Athill's translation of de Pougy helped clarify key passages; Andrea Weiss's work on women in Paris was a great overview; and Diana Souhami's work brought fresh insights to my work. There are many others, and I am very grateful.

Finally, I would like to thank my family, the unsung heroes, for supporting me every step along the way and helping to bring this book to fruition. My heart is with you.

Introduction

MELANIE C. HAWTHORNE

In the last few decades, the place of women in modernism has undergone a major reappraisal that has reconfigured the paradigm of that movement itself. Where previously the only woman writer of the period who was admitted to the circle of high modernists was Gertrude Stein, recent histories of modernism have accorded a much wider role for women both as founders and practitioners of the movement. France has begun to rediscover the work of Claude Cahun (Lucy Schwob, 1894–1954) and Mireille Havet (1898–1932). In the United States, a landmark publication in this reshaping of the field was of course Sandra Gilbert and Susan Gubar's monumental three-volume study *No Man's Land: The Place of the Woman Writer in the Twentieth Century*, which argued (among other things) that gender was not simply ancillary to modernism, a curious sidebar that could be consulted or ignored at will, but one of the foundational impulses fueling modernist expression and experimentation (see in particular volume 2, *Sexchanges*).[1] Shari Benstock's influential synthesis *The Women of the Left Bank* helped shape a vision that brought together a generation of women, both French and Anglophone, as a coherent international movement rather than as a group of individual exceptions.[2] And the work of Bonnie Kime Scott—beginning with the edited collection *The Gender of Modernism* and most notably in the two-volume *Refiguring Modernism*—went one step further and argued that rather than trying to fit women into the male paradigm of modernism, a paradigm that privileged the earlier moment of 1914, women modernists had their own paradigm that matured in the interwar years.[3] More recently still, the study of "sapphic modernism," led by Laura Doan, Jane Garrity, and Tirza True Latimer, has suggested that sexual experimentation was one of the ways women sought to express modernism; in other words, sexuality was not merely a personal matter but was one avenue of aesthetic exploration.[4]

As a result of these sweeping changes in the way modernism has been viewed, the careers and work of numerous women have undergone a reassessment. Women whose writings were, just a few decades ago, marginalized and seldom read or studied are now considered central to the modernist movement; their works are assigned in graduate programs, dissertations are written about them, and—most important—they are being reprinted, read, and discussed. Names that would have been known only to experts a short time ago are now front and center of the field. Probably the greatest success story in this vein is the work of Djuna Barnes, whose work languished mostly out of print or unread just a few decades ago, yet who now is studied as one of the most creative and rewarding of the modernists. Her most celebrated novel, *Nightwood* (1936), originally prefaced but also pruned by T. S. Eliot, has found a new generation of appreciative readers and has even been republished in its original (uncensored) form with related critical apparatus.[5] Barnes has been the subject of serious, scholarly biographies (most notably in works by Andrew Field and Phillip Herring), as well as of anthologies of critical readings (such as *Silence and Power*, edited by Mary Lynn Broe), not to mention general studies and dissertations.[6] Much of Barnes's work—early short stories, poems such as *The Book of Repulsive Women*, plays such as *The Antiphon*, and her early journalism—have returned to print. A volume of *Collected Poems* was published in 2005, and even her artwork has received critical acclaim.[7] These publications demonstrate that the peaks of Barnes's oeuvre, such as *Nightwood*, were but the tip of a vast but hitherto submerged iceberg, and have rendered the sheer mass of that output more visible and available for critical treatment. Natalie Barney's work is just as diverse, as we are now beginning to appreciate, and the publication of the present translation restores one more piece to her own vast creative enterprise.

Today's readers are fortunate that works such as Djuna Barnes's *Ladies Almanack*, at one time considered impenetrable and obscure, are once again appreciated now that they can be read—or re-read—in their proper context, that of a roman à clef about a modernist coterie of women writers. An important member of that coterie, one who facilitated the work of many others, and the central character of *Ladies Almanack*, is Natalie Barney. Natalie Clifford Barney was born in Dayton, Ohio, on October 31, 1876, the daughter of Alice Pike Barney (1857–1931), a society woman with artistic aspirations, and Albert Clifford Barney (1850–1902), a somewhat more staid industrialist who had made a fortune in the railroad business. In late nineteenth-century America, the nouveaux riches of the United States looked longingly at the old money of Europe, where an established— and preferably aristocratic—name was the one thing money could not buy (except through marriage). As a result, European culture exerted a strong pull on America's wealthiest families, who used their money to travel frequently to, maintain residences in, and spend extended periods of time in Europe in general and Paris in particular, Paris being one of the most glittering and vibrant cities at the turn of the century. The Barney family had an impressive home in Bar Harbor, Maine, for domestic vacations, but Natalie Barney's family was also typical of its wealthy generation in looking to Europe for cultural fulfillment. The result was that, from an early age, Natalie learned to speak French and felt at home in France.

In addition to receiving private tutoring, Natalie was educated at an exclusive French school for girls just outside Paris: Les Ruches. It seems more than a matter of mere coincidence that this school is the setting for the lesbian cult classic *Olivia*, originally published anonymously by Virginia Woolf's Hogarth Press in 1949 and now regularly reprinted as a staple of lesbian literature. This novel was in fact written by Dorothy Strachey Bussy, a member of the culturally influential Strachey family (the biographer of eminent Victorians, Lytton Strachey, was her brother); she later became the English translator of French novelist André Gide.[8] *Olivia* was loosely based on her experiences as a pupil in the hothouse atmosphere of the school and portrays the complex web of affective relationships, infatuations, and crushes that link the headmistress, the teachers, and the pupils themselves. This was the atmosphere in which the young Natalie spent her formative years. (Curiously, Les Ruches was also the alma mater of First-Lady-to-be Eleanor Roosevelt, though she was not part of Barney's cohort.)

After such a childhood, it comes as no surprise that Barney never quite succeeded in tearing herself away from France (not that she wanted to), and for the remainder of her life Paris provided her home base. While she spent extended periods of time away—on frequent and regular vacations, on visits to the United States, and even as an exile in Italy during World War II—France was her adopted home, and her address at 20 rue Jacob in the heart of the Left Bank of Paris became legendary.

Here, Natalie Barney hosted a famous salon that flourished particularly during the interwar years (1919–39), and it is often as a hostess that Barney has been remembered since her death in 1972. Her salon brought together writers from Britain, France, and the United States (as well as other countries), thereby providing multiple opportunities for the international movement that was modernism to cross-pollinate. The enterprise took place under the sign of friendship, emblematized by the *temple à l'amitié* (temple to friendship), a small classical-style urban folly that stood in the courtyard. But Barney's reputation as society figure, while immensely important, has been allowed to eclipse the fact that she was also a noted writer in her own right. Indeed, when she died (still in Paris, though exiled from the rue Jacob) at the age of 94, it was first and foremost as an author that she was recalled in the obituary that appeared in the *New York Times* on February 3, 1972. "Natalie Barney, Author, 94, Dies" read the headline, followed by a subheading, "Host to Literary Giants in Paris Was Also Translator." The announcement summarized—and ranked—the three reasons Barney was to be remembered: first as an author in her own right; then as the host of the famous salon (Ernest Hemingway, Marcel Proust, and James Joyce are evoked in the following paragraph of the obituary); and finally as a translator. Alas, despite the suggestion by the *New York Times* (whose informant was the late Herbert Lottman) that Barney was first and foremost an author, she has not always been remembered

in this capacity.[9] Her role as salon hostess has become the stuff of legend, and her social connections to the literary lions of modernism has
long been recognized, but her own contributions to modernism and the
international waves that shaped it have been vastly underrated.

There are a number of reasons her work has so often been overlooked
in the past. To begin with, much of the work she chose to publish during her lifetime is in a genre that does not speak to the Anglophone
world and its contemporary literary traditions. Her preferred genre was
the aphorism, or pensée. Literally (and literarily), a pensée is a thought,
an insight into human nature or life that derives its style from concise,
incisive expression and rhetorical finesse. It is a genre much appreciated
in the Francophone tradition, where the most celebrated collection of
pensées was authored by the philosopher Blaise Pascal (1623–62) and
published posthumously in 1670.[10] The genre was subsequently refined
and extended by notable authors such as the Duke de la Rochefoucauld
(1630–80) in his *Maximes* (definitive edition 1678), and by the *moraliste*
and philosopher Jean de La Bruyère (1645–96) in his *Caractères* (first published in 1688). The epigrammatic style of the aphorism has never
enjoyed such a strong foothold in Anglophone writing, though it is
worth recalling that its most celebrated practitioner in English was Oscar
Wilde (whom Barney once met as a child), whose wit continues to be
appreciated and cited for its pithiness. Even in France, however, Barney's
preference for brevity and a genre associated with seventeenth-century
"golden age" classicism was out of fashion in the talkative and prolix age
that valued Marcel Proust and *Ulysses*, the roman-fleuve series, and multi-
volume works such as Jean-Paul Sartre's *Les chemins de la liberté* and John
Dos Passos's *U.S.A.*

The second reason Barney has been underappreciated is that her work
can seem improvisational and unfinished. It has often been stated that
Barney seldom revised her work, the implication being that she was not
serious about her writing. It is true that part of the appeal of the apho-
ristic style is that it should appear light and spontaneous, but anyone
who has thought for more than a few minutes about this form must
realize that although such an impression of ease is an essential part of

the work, the actual composition requires much more effort than can appear in the final product.[11] To be successful, an epigram must not seem forced, but if the "bon mot" is to have its rhetorical effect, much more thought—if not always revision on the page—must go into its writing than may be allowed to show. The aphorism must disguise its labor if it is to succeed.

In any case, the stereotype that Barney did not spend much time revising her work is easily belied by a study of her letters. Here there is plenty of evidence to suggest that she cared very deeply about composition and its effects. A striking example of her concern with revision comes from her (unpublished) correspondence with the artist Romaine Brooks.[12] Brooks was Barney's lover and longtime companion from approximately 1916 until just before Brooks's death in 1970 (including the period when the events represented in *Amants féminins* were unfolding; indeed, while Brooks is not named in the novel, she is evoked). In one particular instance of the letters, in a response to stinging criticism from Brooks, there are several drafts of the same letter from Barney, showing how she reworked what she wanted to say. Like the aphorism, the letter is a genre that appears spontaneous and unstudied, but in both cases the finished product does not always retain the traces of the effort that went into its production. In Barney's case, then, it is possible to argue that the apparent lightness of much of her writing is a studied effect rather than the result of lack of care in composition. The idea that she dashed off her work without much thought is a myth that merits revision.

The third reason Barney's work has remained undervalued is because so much of it still remains either unpublished altogether or untranslated into English. Barney's claim to literary fame has long rested on just a handful of publications, most of which have remained perennial favorites among those familiar with her work but have not yet attained wider popularity. During her lifetime, Barney published mostly in French (the language she adopted along with her residence) beginning with her first publication in 1900—a small edition of poetry entitled *Quelques portraits-sonnets de femmes*—and ending with the 1963 *Traits et portraits*.[13] Only one work was originally published in English, *The One Who Is Legion; or, A.D.'s*

After-Life.[14] Over the years, a number of her works have been reissued or reprinted in France. This modest but steady stream is testimony to her enduring popularity among connoisseurs. It is notable, too, that there has even been an audience for her work *in French* in the United States, where the Arno Press of New York reprinted both *Aventures de l'esprit* and *Traits et portraits* in 1975.

The history of the republication of Barney's work (either in France or in the United States) tells its own story, too: clearly the interest in Barney began to revive and grow after her death in 1972. The Arno reprints in 1975 were part of a larger project sparked by the gay liberation movement to make key texts by gay and lesbian authors available to a new audience hungry to rediscover this suppressed tradition of literature. Here Barney's oeuvre can be placed alongside that of other gay and lesbian writers whose work was long shunned but is now considered canonical. Radclyffe Hall's *The Well of Loneliness*, for example, has become a core text of undergraduate survey courses (of women's writing, gay and lesbian writing, and even modernism), and openness to seeing the value of once-proscribed works has created a new audience for Barney.

Barney's work has also maintained a faithful following among academics, and the last three decades have seen a slow but steady increase in the number of reprints and reissues of her work in French. This trend began with *Un panier de framboises* in 1979, *Eparpillements* in 1982, and *Souvenirs indiscrets* in 1983. The flow continued in the 1990s with *Aventures de l'esprit* in 1992, *Nouvelles pensées de l'Amazone* in 1996, and *Quelques portraits-sonnets de femmes* in 1999. The present century has already seen a reissue of *Traits et portraits* (2002), and one hopes that more is to follow.

What has not always been available are good translations of Barney's books for Anglophone readers. While the Arno editions mentioned above made available the French version of her work, only two volumes of translation into English have appeared to date, both in 1992. An anthology subtitled "The Best of Natalie Clifford Barney" brought together excerpts in English from a range of Barney's publications, but the only translation of a *complete* work to date remains *Adventures of the Mind* (a translation of *Aventures de l'esprit*), published by New York University Press.[15]

The present volume, then, makes a hitherto unknown work available in English (the work was only just published for the first time anywhere— in the original French—in 2013), so that contemporary scholars can begin to reassess Barney's relationship to modernism and her peer writers. The general studies of modernism cited in the opening paragraphs, along with the extensive studies reevaluating individual writers, have all contributed to a new perspective on modernism, one that in turn provides the framework for a reassessment of Barney and her oeuvre. For while Barney lived a long and productive life, and was actively publishing before modernism emerged and after it had waned, her main literary contributions were composed during the heyday of modernism and under its star of influence. The present work, *Women Lovers, or The Third Woman*, dates from 1926, for example (as a note inside the cover of the manuscript states). Bonnie Kime Scott privileges the year 1928 as being of special importance for modernist women, since it saw the publication of so many memorable works (Virginia Woolf's *Orlando*, Radclyffe Hall's *The Well of Loneliness*, and Djuna Barnes's *Ladies Almanack*, to name but three). Barney's autobiographical novel falls just shy of that peak date (though had the work been published in Barney's lifetime, 1928 might very well have been the year it would have appeared in print), but in its themes, its forms, and its preoccupations, the novel shares many features of the work by Barney's contemporaries of this period: Woolf, Hall, and Barnes.

The source material for the novel is an autobiographical episode that Barney experienced around the time of composition. The facts of the matter are as follows: Barney's friend and ex-lover Liane de Pougy, one of the most celebrated courtesans of the Belle Epoque, was experiencing marital problems.[16] Pougy had married Prince Ghika (acquiring her own royal title of "princess" in so doing), but the match had not put an end to other romantic attachments by both parties. In a stunning irony that could only happen in real life, the prince had run off with his wife's young (female) lover, and Liane had been transformed from the one having the adulterous affair into the aggrieved and abandoned party.

Natalie Barney was a famously loyal friend (she once stated that once her friendship was given, she never took it back). Barney's willingness to help those in distress is also a quality celebrated (albeit tongue in cheek) by her friend Djuna Barnes in her *Ladies Almanack.* Those familiar with Barnes's work already know that the central character of the *Almanack,* Dame Evangeline Musset, is based on Natalie Barney. In Barnes's depiction, Evangeline Musset, famous for her "slips of the tongue" (which here takes on a double meaning), helps young girls in (romantic) distress or, as Barnes more poetically puts it, is "one Grand Red Cross for the Pursuance, the Relief and the Distraction, of such Girls as in their Hinder Parts, and the Fore Parts, and in whatsoever Parts did suffer them most, lament Cruelly."[17] The description of Barney as a one-woman relief organization for the disappointed in love, a sort of lesbian Red Cross, captures the benevolent intentions that led to the events recounted in Barney's own novel *Amants féminins,* and the publication of Natalie Barney's version of events thus has a collateral benefit in that it also sheds light on the circumstances that inspired Djuna Barnes's extraordinary and witty masterpiece.[18]

Ever the loyal friend, then, Barney was determined to distract the abandoned Liane de Pougy from her emotional distress, and what better way than to offer Pougy a new love interest. At the time, Barney had recently begun a new affair with Mimi Franchetti. It wasn't a particularly serious affair. Barney once offered a list of her primary relationships, divided into *liaisons* (serious relationships), *demi-liaisons* (semi-serious affairs), and *aventures* (flings). The relationship with Pougy counted as a serious affair, but Mimi Franchetti is mentioned only as an *aventure.*[19] In any case, Barney was famous for her rejection of monogamy and jealousy, qualities she found unattractive and irrelevant, and during the time she became involved with Franchetti and Pougy (the latter for the second time), she was also in a long-term relationship with Romaine Brooks and in a similarly long-term relationship with Elisabeth de Gramont, this last a commitment Barney considered a marriage, though not one that required fidelity.[20] Confident that the fling with Franchetti was no more than a pleasant interlude, Barney invited Pougy to share her bed and her new lover in a three-way relationship that quickly got out of hand. Barney found herself hoist by her own petard, mired in an ugly jealousy, and deprived of

her lover, who took to Pougy with an unanticipated attachment, thus
leaving Barney out in the cold. A lesson in love, then, for one who
thought she was above them, and a revelation about her own capacity to
experience jealousy, possessiveness, and emotional avarice.

So much for the events inspiring the novel and some of the themes it
takes up. What marks the novel as an example of modernism, however, is
the experimental aspect of both its themes and forms. To begin with, the
novel challenges thematic taboos through its depiction of lesbian sexuality as grounded in physical expression. This subject had mostly been
limited to pornographic texts for a male audience until the twentieth
century, so to take such a subject out of the realm of pornography and
resituate it as part of an investigation of human emotion breaks new
ground. This challenging of taboos is consistent with many other modernist texts of the era, works that Barney knew well. Radclyffe Hall's *The
Well of Loneliness* has already been cited (as one of the landmark publications of 1928), and of course Natalie Barney appears in a cameo role
in that novel under the name Valerie Seymour. *The Well of Loneliness* was
famously banned (in England; it was subsequently printed in France),
despite a trial in which Virginia Woolf was prepared to take the stand
in defense of the novel. Through her association with publisher Sylvia
Beach, another "woman of the Left Bank," Barney was also familiar with
the controversial publication history of James Joyce's *Ulysses* (and indeed
Joyce himself was also an habitué of Barney's salon). *Ulysses* challenged
taboos; *Ulysses* was banned. The depiction of unacceptable forms of sexuality had also caused the censure of D. H. Lawrence's *Lady Chatterley's Lover*.
These are but a handful of the works that pushed the limits of what kinds
of sexuality could acceptably be represented in fiction (same-sex, mastur-
batory, cross-class), and Barney was no doubt encouraged by this contes-
tatory atmosphere to add her own contribution to the voices of challenge.
Rather than stifle her sexuality and only hint at the physical dimension of
the relationship (which was how some other writers avoided censorship),
Barney places her characters' sexuality at the center of her work. Arguably,
since the work remained unpublished, Barney may have fallen victim to
the most insidious form of censorship of all, that of self-censorship,

and since Barney decided not to pursue publication of *Amants féminins*, the courageous impulse not to mute her representation of women's passion in her composition has been overlooked until now. But at least in retrospect it becomes possible to appreciate the courage it took to commit such things to paper, and the novel contributes to a deeper appreciation of women's modernism of the 1920s.

In her themes, then, Barney explores women's emotional and sexual independence from men, a subject much in the air even before World War I, but a theme that took on newer relevance and greater urgency after it (one thinks of the controversial novel *La garçonne* by Victor Margueritte, among others).[21] The boldness of Barney's work can be measured when set alongside Hall's *The Well of Loneliness*, a contemporary work lionized for its groundbreaking depiction of lesbianism. In Hall's novel, despite its boldness, there is a tone of apology, an implicit acceptance of the medicalized definition of lesbianism as deviant and pathological, and finally a sense of shame. Barney offers no such compromising language. Women's love for each other is normalized, the definitions imposed by society are irrelevant, and if it is true that the course of true love does not run smooth in her novel, still the complications derive from unexpectedly universal human emotions, such as jealousy, and not from decadent notions of morbidity inherent in "deviant" forms of sexuality that must be seen to be punished.

Barney not only defends "deviant" sexuality, she goes far beyond her contemporaries in proposing a revision of the usual understanding of the sex and gender categories. Perhaps it is testimony to the far-reaching influence of Simone de Beauvoir's *The Second Sex*, but there persists today a largely unexamined assumption that women are the "second sex" in the same way that they have historically been second-class citizens, men being implicitly both the first class and sex. And in this paradigm, the third sex is left to that class of people who are neither fully men nor women, those who feel they do not, cannot, fit into one or the other of the two sex categories. Members of the third sex are not even a class; they are simply a collection of outcasts. Barney explicitly invokes this third sex category but in such a way as to challenge and rewrite the usual twentieth- and twenty-first-century understanding and hierarchy of the sexes. A glance at other references to the "third sex" among Barney's contemporaries illustrates how that term was generally understood at the time. The sexologist Magnus Hirschfeld used the title *The Third Sex* for his study of Berlin's homosexuals (1908), and this is the same meaning found in the "gay guide" *The Third Sex* published by Willy in 1927.[22] Willy, the ex-husband of writer Colette (another of Barney's conquests), was no doubt not the sole author of the work (he excelled at employing ghostwriters), but the title of this overview of Paris-Sodom underscores the perception that at the time when Barney was writing her novel, "the third sex" was widely understood to refer to gay or homosexual people, effeminate men, and masculine women.

But *Amants féminins* reminds us of another, more ancient tradition, one that dates from Greek antiquity, a tradition that inspired pioneering sexual reformers of the nineteenth century such as Karl Heinrich Ulrichs but was subsequently brushed aside by the likes of Hirschfeld. To understand this older paradigm, it is necessary to return to a reading of the philosopher Plato. In his *Symposium* (also sometimes translated as *The Banquet*), Aristophanes undertakes to explain to the intellectual elite of Athens the origin of sexual desire. According to the founding myth that he retells, there *used to be* three sexes: male, female, and androgynous (having elements of both). So far so good, this corresponds to what we think of as the three sex/gender categories today. But in reading this myth we must take into account the fundamental nature of each of these beings, because originally, the story goes, they were *all* double beings. "Each person's shape was complete," we are told. "They were round, with their backs and sides forming a circle. They had four hands and the same number of legs, and two absolutely identical faces on a cylindrical neck. They had a single head for their two faces (which were on opposite sides), four ears, two sets of genitals, and every other part of their bodies was how you'd imagine it on the basis of what I've said."[23]

These creatures were so strong and proud, however, that the gods found it necessary to punish them, to cut them down to size, as it were. But how? Zeus came up with the solution by cutting each creature in half. Since those times, human beings have forgotten that this was their original state, but what remains is a desire to be reunited with their other half, to merge again into one entity, and this, maintains Aristophanes, is what we have come to think of as sexual desire. But this explanation means that a man who was formerly part of an entirely male being will seek to reunite with a man, a woman who was attached to another female will again seek a female, and so on: "Any women who are offcuts from the female gender aren't particularly interested in men; they incline more towards women, and therefore female homosexuals come from this group. And any men who are offcuts from the male gender go for males," explains Aristophanes.[24]

In this scheme of things, the beings who are most completely male or female (they were once part of a creature that was 100 percent male or female) are, in their current, cloven form, *homosexual* in their desire; indeed, their desire is the proof of their deeply rooted gender identity. Only members of the third sex, originally of mixed or androgynous sex (a man originally combined with a woman, having both kinds of genitals), are *heterosexual* in their present state, the masculine half seeking a feminine half in order to complete itself. So if we retain the perspective of Aristophanes, the first sex consists of men seeking men (as the personal ads would phrase it today), while the second (pace Beauvoir) would be lesbians (rather than all women as a class).[25] The third sex would consist of the people considered "normal" (in the sense that they are heterosexual) in twentieth-century terms, but their sexual orientation stems from a fundamentally androgynous nature that the twentieth century would view as deviant.

If Barney proposes yet a different definition of the third sex, it is nevertheless one that is grafted on to the Platonic understanding of human beings as originally a couple, a fused twosome. She brings out this philosophy in the novel in the self-portrait she paints of "N.," when she writes that "N. belongs to that category of people that may become less rare when the age-old earthly couple is definitively discredited, permitting each person to keep or rediscover her own wholeness" (16; "N. appartient à une catégorie d'êtres dont l'espèce deviendra peut-être moins rare lorsque le vieux couple terrestre, définitivement discrédité, permettra à chacun de garder ou de retrouver son entité"). This category, the "third one [sex]" consists of those men and women who are whole in and of themselves, those who do not need another half to complete them. Which is not to say that they are sexless or misanthropic loners, since they want to connect to an other, but without becoming fused with that person into a single unit. "This third woman is not looking for her other half or someone to complete her, but a twin—a 'companion in love'—a variation of her kind" (17; "Cette troisième ne cherche pas un complément, un conjoint, mais un semblable—un 'compagnon d'amour'—une variété de son espèce"). For Natalie Barney, the first two sexes account for the majority of humans (though she is not explicit about how, exactly), but members of the third sex are defined not by their sexual orientation (the group accommodates everyone from homosexual men and women to angels[26]) but by their orientation vis-à-vis the need to form a couple: their search—or lack of it—for completion.

Natalie Barney is not the only author to propose an innovative definition of the third sex in these opening decades of the twentieth century. As early as 1890 a novel had appeared with the title *Le troisième sexe* (The third sex). The author was a Belgian woman, largely forgotten today, by the name of Marguerite Coppin, and her novel was considered provocative enough in its title that the authorities began an inquiry into its immorality. Had they taken the trouble to read the novel, however, they might have learned that what they took to be a reference to (female) homosexuality was in fact something entirely different. In the age of decadence that privileged the cerebral, what Coppin had in mind was a perverse form of love that was purely intellectual, in which physical feelings played no part, regardless of the sex and/or gender of the lovers.

Coppin was not alone in exploring and proposing alternative definitions. The work of Renée Vivien (Pauline Tarn, 1877–1909), particularly her roman à clef novel *Une femme m'apparut* (there are two versions, 1904 and 1905), also explores a third sex. Vivien, who lived through a tumultuous relationship with Barney that marked her for life, represents Barney in the work(s) under the name of Flossie or Valley (depending on which version is consulted) but also created a sort of alter ego figure who borrows "his" appearance from Leonardo da Vinci's androgynous John the Baptist figure. This wise person is not so much a blend of both sexes as a disembodied sexless consciousness, anticipating the sexless figure of the angel who looks human but is above and beyond matters of the flesh.

Yet another variation on the theme of the third sex comes from another of Barney's contemporaries and acquaintances, Claude Cahun, whose work (as mentioned above) has begun to draw widespread attention following a major retrospective of her career. Cahun emphasized what she called (in French) the *neutre*. In her surrealist book of fragmented musings *Aveux non avenus* (translated as *Disavowals*) published in 1930 (i.e., around the same time as the composition of *Amants féminins*), Cahun wonders where she fits on the sex/gender continuum: "Masculine? Feminine? It depends on the situation. Neuter is the only gender that always suits me."[27] This third category into which Cahun places herself is not quite "neuter" in the sense of the impotently de-sexed (the way castration "neuters" an animal) so much as it represents a (gender) neutral or asexual category, one that contains not *both* sexes the way "hermaphrodite" or "androgyne" do, but rather *neither* sex. For Cahun, the third sex refuses the blend of androgyny in order to create a category that escapes or exceeds the binary of traditional sex categories altogether.

Speculation about the exact nature of the third sex was thus part of the cultural wallpaper of Barney's world, and agreement on what there might be beyond the options of "man/male" and "woman/female" was far from established. Barney's novel should be seen as part of this larger conversation, and it reminds us furthermore that definition of the third sex has strayed far from its Platonic origins despite whatever claims to that authority may be made.

Barney, it turns out, was a queer theorist *avant la lettre*, but the thematic innovations of her novel are also matched by its formal qualities. The novel opens with a list of dramatis personae in which a word portrait of each character is presented in alphabetical order (L., M., N.). It is all too easy to understand these initials as standing for Liane, Mimi, and Natalie, so it is hardly credible to conclude that Barney thought she was disguising the identity of the characters by using this technique. Rather, by reducing the characters to mere letters, a cipher, Barney is emphasizing their standing as fictional creations rather than real people. Each of the characters is a role and is not meant to be simply a portrayal of the real person who inspired the events. Rather than introduce characters and let the reader develop a sense of who they are by showing them react and grow, Barney offers a brief description of each person, summarizing their character and temperament.

After this setting of the scene, the novel comprises three parts: "Notes from N.'s Journal," "Written in the Third Person," and "N. Takes Up Her Travel Diaries Again." Barney experiments with different narrative voices, blending first-person and third-person perspectives. She also incorporates different genres throughout the novel. The verbal portraits of the characters consist of an accretion of nominal phrases, with little attempt to link the observations with verbs. Also, Barney's penchant for aphorism is evident from beginning to end. The very first sentence of the novel, the beginning of the portrait of L. (Liane de Pougy), consists of a verbless juxtaposition of opposites that summarizes the generosity and shortcomings of Pougy's character as well as her life's trajectory (she would end her days as a tertiary [lay] member of a Dominican order of nuns): "The great courtesan, the little saint" (9; "La grande courtisane, la petite sainte"). A pendant to this opening "thought," the very last sentence of the novel summarizes the plot and the lesson to be drawn from it with the maxim "The worst isn't that we burn ourselves, but that the fire goes out" (160; "Le pire n'est pas que l'on se brûle, mais que le feu s'éteint"). In between, Barney gathers conventional narrative along with poems, letters, social announcements (*faire-parts*), extracts from diaries, and dialogues to create an impression of a narrative assembled from fragments and told through collage. Barney echoes experiments in narrative perspective that can be found in the work of modernists such as William Faulkner, for example, and the work of visual artists (Pablo Picasso, the surrealists) who made collages out of everyday scraps of paper. Occasionally, such as when Barney is discussing "several types of third ones," she abandons

conventional linguistic notation altogether and simply draws in the kind
of symbols she is referring to, using pictures rather than words (86).
Such a decentered narrative rejects the authority of a single narrative
voice, and indeed Barney rejects closure in her final statement: "END
(but there is no end . . .)" (160; "FIN [mais il n'y a pas de fin . . .]").

One of the most striking genres incorporated into the novel is that of
the film script, surely an unusual departure in 1926. This form is evident
in the opening section presenting the characters. As mentioned above,
this section clearly borrows something from the conventions of theater,
but it is apparent from subsequent references that it is not a play that
Barney has in mind here but a film script. To be sure, Barney presents
psychological analysis in a way that owes more (once again) to the seventeenth-century prose of, for example, Madame de Lafayette's *La Princesse
de Clèves*, analysis that is only possible in a written form that can present
the inner thoughts and self-observations of a character, but this psychological realism is combined with a strong sense of the visual as well as
with a consciousness that the novel evolves as though it were a film. One
of the first chapters of the first section of the novel is explicitly called
"Film," for example, and other references to the work as a film are scat-
tered throughout the novel.

Film was still a genre in its infancy in the 1920s before the advent of
sound (usually dated by the release of *The Jazz Singer* in 1927, just after the
composition of Barney's novel). Partly because of its novelty and partly
because of features unique to the French context, French film at this time,
while still very popular, was more of an "art cinema" than the mass enter-
tainment it would later become.[28] It had not yet developed an extensive
professional class but drew on those involved in other art forms (writers
and visual artists) who lent their talents as a sideline. Barney's salon
attracted people from almost every corner of the art world, from opera
singers and avant-garde composers to poets and polemicists, but few of
these were formally involved in filmmaking. So Barney most likely learned
about scriptwriting from her close friend and sometime lover Colette.
Colette began writing film criticism as early as 1914, and participated in

adapting scenarios of some of her own works for the screen just after
World War I (an engagement that would increase in the 1930s and
beyond).[29] Thanks to her music hall days, Colette was also close to actors
and actresses who would cross over from the stage to the screen as the
movie industry took off. A notable example is the actress Musidora
(Jeanne Roques, 1889–1957), one of the first "vamps" of silent film.[30]
Others include Polaire (Émilie Marie Bouchaud, 1874–1939) and Pola
Negri (Barbara Apolonia Chałupiec, 1897–1987). Another source of information and inspiration for Barney would have been the fortunes of
Lucie Delarue-Mardrus, another of her lovers, who was having two of
her novels adapted for the cinema in the 1920s. Envisaging this possibility for her own work may have led Barney to think in terms of a film
script during the very composition of *Amants féminins* (rather than con-
ceiving of it primarily as a novel that might later be adapted).

Finally, it is necessary to say something about the manuscript. The
novel consists of 145 typed, double-spaced pages, including a table of
contents, with occasional corrections and emendations (which appear
to be in a hand other than Barney's, according to the publisher of the
French edition, Yvan Quintin). Handwritten inside the front cover is the
information that *Amants féminins* was written in 1926 for Mimi Franchetti,
and Barney has appended her signature after the concluding words of
the manuscript, "(mais il n'y a pas de fin . . .)"

There is no real end to such a story, Barney asserts, and it is to be
hoped that there is no end to Barney and her story either, at least no end
to interest in and discussion of her work. The publication of this novel,
some forty years after Barney's death, is both a testimony to that enduring interest and an attempt to prolong the story.

NOTES

1. Sandra Gilbert and Susan Gubar, *No Man's Land: The Place of the Woman Writer
in the Twentieth Century* (New Haven: Yale University Press, 1988–1994).

2. Shari Benstock, *The Women of the Left Bank* (Austin: University of Texas Press,
1986).

3. Bonnie Kime Scott, ed., *The Gender of Modernism* (Bloomington: Indiana
University Press, 1990); Bonnie Kime Scott, *Refiguring Modernism* (Bloomington:
Indiana University Press, 1995).

4. See, for example, Laura Doan and Jane Garrity, eds., *Sapphic Modernities: Sexuality, Women and National Culture* (New York: Palgrave Macmillan, 2006), and Jasmine Rault, *Eileen Gray and the Design of Sapphic Modernity: Staying In* (Burlington, VT: Ashgate, 2011). Rault summarizes this perspective on modernism in the following terms: "A growing field of research in the field of sapphic modernity has shown that for women, before the media advent and wide circulation of a stable and criminal lesbian identity, becoming non-heterosexual was synonymous with becoming modern" (4). See also Tirza True Latimer, *Women Together / Women Apart: Portraits of Lesbian Paris* (New Brunswick: Rutgers University Press, 2005), and Whitney Chadwick and Tirza True Latimer, eds., *The Modern Woman Revisited: Paris between the Wars* (New Brunswick: Rutgers University Press, 2003).

5. Djuna Barnes, *Nightwood: The Original Version and Related Drafts*, ed. Cheryl J. Plumb (Chicago: Dalkey Archive Press, 1995).

6. See Andrew Field, *Djuna: The Life and Times of Djuna Barnes* (New York: Putnam, 1983); Phillip Herring, *Djuna: The Life and Work of Djuna Barnes* (New York: Viking, 1995); and Hank O'Neal, *"Life is painful, nasty, and short—in my case it has only been painful and nasty": Djuna Barnes, 1978–1981; An Informal Memoir* (New York: Paragon, 1990). See also Mary Lynn Broe, ed., *Silence and Power: A Reevaluation of Djuna Barnes* (Carbondale: Southern Illinois University Press, 1991).

7. Recent reprints of Barnes's work include *Ryder* (New York: St. Martin's Press, 1979); *Smoke and Other Early Stories*, ed. Douglas Messerli (Los Angeles: Sun and Moon Press, 1982); *Interviews*, ed. Alyce Barry (Los Angeles: Sun and Moon Press, 1985; also republished by Routledge in 2003); *New York*, ed. Alyce Barry, drawings by Djuna Barnes (Los Angeles: Sun and Moon Press, 1989; also republished in London by Virago in 1990); *Ladies Almanack* (Chicago: Dalkey Archive Press, 1992; also republished by Carcanet in 2006); *The Book of Repulsive Women: Eight Rhythms and Five Drawings* (Los Angeles: Sun and Moon Press, 1994); *Poe's Mother: Selected Drawings of Djuna Barnes*, ed. Douglas Messerli (Los Angeles: Sun and Moon Press, 1995); *Nightwood; At the Roots of the Stars: The Short Plays*, ed. Douglas Messerli (Los Angeles: Sun and Moon Press, 1995); *Collected Stories*, ed. Phillip Herring (Los Angeles: Sun and Moon Press, 1996); *The Antiphon* (Los Angeles: Green Integer, 2000); *Collected Poems: With Notes toward the Memoirs*, ed. Phillip Herring and Osías Stutman (Madison: University of Wisconsin Press, 2005); and, most recently, the *Biography of Julie Van Bartmann*, ed. Douglas Messerli (Los Angeles: Green Integer, 2016). One can only hope that the revival of interest in Barney will lead to such a wealth of publications.

8. On the Strachey family, see Barbara Caine, *Bombay to Bloomsbury: A Biography of the Strachey Family* (New York: Oxford University Press, 2005).

9. Lottman, the author of *The Left Bank* and numerous biographies of leading twentieth-century French intellectuals, was known for his rigor and for avoiding overreliance on anecdote. He died in 2014.

10. Pascal's appreciation of brevity is such that he is said to have apologized to a correspondent for writing such a long letter but "he didn't have time for a short one." I am grateful to LeAnn Fields for this anecdote.

11. In the first edition of *Une femme m'apparut* (Paris: Alphonse Lemerre, 1904), Renée Vivien implies that Barney mocked writers who strove for a "natural" style in their writing. All they had to do, claimed Barney, was leave the spelling and punctuation mistakes—the most natural thing in the world—in their manuscripts.

12. The papers are preserved at the McFarlin Library, University of Tulsa, Tulsa, Oklahoma.

13. *Quelques portraits-sonnets de femmes* was recently reissued in a facsimile edition (Verona: L'Amazone retrouvée, 1999). *Eparpillements* (Paris: Sansot, 1910) was reprinted in 1982 by Persona (Paris). *Nouvelles pensées de l'Amazone* (Paris: Mercure de France, 1939) was reprinted by Ivrea (Paris) in 1996. *Souvenirs indiscrets* (Paris: Flammarion, 1960) was reissued in 1983, while *Traits et portraits* (Paris: Mercure de France, 1963) was reissued in 2002.

14. *The One Who Is Legion; or, A.D.'s After-Life* was published in London by Partridge in 1930. One work was published simultaneously in English and French: *Poems & Poèmes: Autres alliances*, published both in Paris by Emile-Paul and in New York by Doran in 1920.

15. *A Perilous Advantage: The Best of Natalie Clifford Barney*, ed. Anna Livia (Vermont: New Victoria Publishers of Norwich, 1992). *Adventures of the Mind*, trans. John Spalding Gatton (New York: New York University Press, 1992).

16. On Liane de Pougy, see Jean Chalon, *Liane de Pougy: Courtisane, princesse et sainte* (Paris: Flammarion, 1994). Biographies of Barney such as Suzanne Rodriguez's *Wild Heart: A Life: Natalie Clifford Barney's Journey from Victorian America to the Literary Salons of Paris* (New York: HarperCollins, 2002) and Diana Souhami's *Wild Girls* (London: Weidenfeld and Nicolson, 2004) contain accounts of Barney's affair with Liane de Pougy, which is also fictionalized in Pougy's novel *Idylle saphique*, first published in 1901. The novel has yet to be translated into English, but Pougy's diaries, translated by Diana Athill, were published under the title *My Blue Notebooks* (New York: Harper & Row, 1979). On Barney, see also Karla Jay, *The Amazon and the Page: Natalie Clifford Barney and Renée Vivien* (Bloomington: Indiana University Press, 1988).

17. Barnes, *Ladies Almanack*, 6.

18. Among other things, Barney's novel shows that Barnes, who was experiencing difficulties in her relationship with Thelma Wood, was one of Barney's confidantes and the two spent time commiserating when things went wrong.

19. See Francesco Rapazzini, *Elisabeth de Gramont: Avant-gardiste* (Paris: Fayard, 2004), 491.

20. In his biography of de Gramont, Rapazzini gives a transcript of the marriage contract, a document drawn up by Barney in June 1920 that opens with the specific words "contrat de marriage" (marriage contract) (*Elisabeth de Gramont*,

340–42). Though without any legal force, the contract was voluntarily accepted by both parties and lasted until de Gramont died in 1954. The contract acknowledges that both parties are likely to be tempted by *aventures* (flings), and imposes no promises of fidelity, only a commitment that each party shall undertake to bring the other back to the union ("il suffira que l'un ramène l'autre à lui . . . parcequ'union oblige").

21. For more on the controversy surrounding the changing social and sexual roles of women—and the reactions against them in post–World War I France—see Mary Louise Roberts, *Civilization without Sexes* (Chicago: University of Chicago Press, 1994).

22. A translation by the late—and much missed—Lawrence Schehr was published by the University of Illinois Press in 2007.

23. Plato, *Symposium* (New York: Oxford University Press, 1994), 25. This edition is a recent translation by Robin Waterfield, which offers certain advantages over older translations, though he consistently uses the word "gender" to translate what seem to be references to "sex category" (a person's biological sex as determined principally by sex organs).

24. Ibid., 28.

25. Plato's Greek is rendered different ways by different translators, sometimes as "female homosexuals," sometimes "lesbians" or "tribades," etc. Waterfield notes that "this is the only extant reference in classical Greek literature to female homosexuality" (81), so in a way, all translations introduce an inevitable element of anachronism.

26. On the use of angels to represent androgyny in the work of modernist writers—including Barney—see Suzanne Hobson, *Angels of Modernism: Religion, Culture, Aesthetics 1910–1960* (New York: Palgrave Macmillan, 2011). Hobson focuses on Barney's *The One Who Is Legion*.

27. Claude Cahun, *Disavowals*, trans. Susan de Muth (Cambridge: MIT Press, 2007), 151.

28. Alan Williams, *Republic of Images: A History of French Filmmaking* (Cambridge: Harvard University Press, 1992), 131.

29. See Alain Virmaux and Odette Virmaux, eds., *Colette at the Movies* (New York: Frederick Ungar, 1980). In 1932, Colette would provide the French adaptation of the lesbian film classic *Maedchen in Uniform* that described the kind of schoolgirl passions that Barney had experienced in her school days at Les Ruches.

30. Colette's letters to Musidora were recently published. See Colette, *Un bien grand amour: Lettres à Musidora, 1908–1953* (Paris: L'Herne, 2014).

Translator's Essay

CHELSEA RAY

Works of art are sustained by betrayals in love. After the art of the flesh, works of art.

—NATALIE CLIFFORD BARNEY, *Pensées d'une Amazone*

When I was working in the archives of the Bibliothèque Littéraire Jacques Doucet in Paris during a year of research in 2001, I had the rookie ambition of setting my eyes on everything that Natalie Clifford Barney had left in 1968 under the stewardship of François Chapon, the director of the Bibliothèque.[1] While I did manage to read most of the 167 manuscripts located there, I had a tip about the novel in your hands today: *Women Lovers, or The Third Woman*. I was lucky enough to be working at the library alongside Suzanne Rodriguez, who was completing research for *Wild Heart: A Life: Natalie Clifford Barney's Journey from Victorian America to the Literary Salons of Paris*, her biography that would be published in 2002. She had already seen the manuscript of *Women Lovers* and suggested that I look at it, so it was with great attention that I turned to reading it for the first time. According to Rodriguez's biography, the portrayal "shows a Natalie that few believed possible. Far from being the implacable Amazon always invincible in love, she was simply a woman ripped apart by jealousy and heartbreak."[2] In a similar vein, close friend and biographer Jean Chalon recently commented: "This novel revealed to me a Natalie that I didn't know existed: jealous, impulsive, weak: nothing like the Natalie that I knew, who was Olympian—having mastery over herself and others—and strong. She would tell me—I now understand why—'I wasn't always like this with others, the way I am with you.'"[3]

Indeed, this novel holds the potential to stimulate a reenvisioning of Barney, not only as a historical personality but also as a writer. *Women Lovers* stands apart from most of her other writings because it integrates a kind of Baudelairean decadence into a modernist, experimental novel.[4] The translation in your hands today follows on the heels of the publication of the novel in its original French by ErosOnyx Éditions in 2013.[5] In this brief essay, I hope to show how the central issues of the novel, most notably Barney's philosophy of love and the figure of "the third woman" (*la troisième*), are intricately intertwined with challenges of translation. I will use my own literary interpretation of aspects of the novel as a way of entering into my discussion about choices made in the translation process.

The irony of being an American translating an American did not escape me. Unlike Natalie Barney, I was not exposed to French at a young age, as I did not hear a word of French before my sophomore year in high school. Barney was steeped in the language from a young age and attended the French school Les Ruches.[6] The act of translating this novel caused me to revisit Barney's status as a bilingual writer and evaluate her adoption of French as her literary language. In the preface to *Quelques portraits-sonnets de femmes* (1900), Barney explains:

> I did not write this book in your language out of any kind of pretension; rather, it is because I think poetically only in French. I have such little knowledge of it that I have kept all my illusions about it. I have always instinctively had a kind of artificiality that forces me to debase all that is dear to me; I have lived my day-to-day life in English for so long that it no longer holds any kind of sentimentality for me. In moments of elation, I am deluded into believing that my soul may be a tomb for several French poets.[7]

For Barney, English was the language of daily life, and French was infused with a kind of poetic "sentimentality" she channeled into her writing.

Barney's relationship to French, however, is more complex than the above playful quip would suggest. In reading, interpreting, and translating the novel with the help of native French speakers, I began more clearly to see the challenges inherent in the act of translating a nonnative speaker's literary works. French speakers needed to explain to me where the French was not exactly "French," as my American ear was not tuned into this level of stylistic and linguistic nuance. Jean-Claude Redonnet, professor emeritus of the Sorbonne University, would simply comment, "C'est du Barney" (That's Barney's style), to indicate where she was, in a sense, creating her own language. In the essay "Translation: The Biography of an Art Form," Alice Kaplan contends that "we translators can love, but we can also see every flaw, every mistaken fact, every awkward transition in the work we are translating."[8] Since Barney's novel never went through final edits for publication (other than two excerpts[9]), I had to carefully guard against the impetus to "fix" awkward sentences. At the same time, I felt a strong pull toward readability, knowing full well that the less-refined texture of some sections would come through in any case. In the final analysis, I tried for a middle ground, preserving some of the "awkwardness" of the unedited manuscript while also creating a novel that would draw in the reader and be a pleasure to read in English.

Readability and stylistic considerations were also a factor in choices concerning verb tense. The novel is narrated primarily in the present tense for events that occurred in the past; this is more commonly done in French than in English (using *le présent de narration*). I decided against translating the entire novel in the present tense, however, and made a distinction between sections of the novel that were more plot-based—that is, that moved the story along—from the sections that were more lyrical in quality or consisted primarily of a philosophical discussion about "the third one." I again attempted to strike a middle ground: the plot-based sections in the past tense give a quicker momentum to the storyline, and the lyrical sections in the present tense retained the quality of immediacy in the original.

The narrative quickly establishes a tension between the chapters narrated in the first person and the third person, and this movement between the two creates intricate scaffolding between the characters, the author, and the narrator. Readers' expectations about a strict separation between the narrator and the author are confounded from the beginning:

> This novel is from N.'s notebooks.
> The scenes and commentary in the third person come from the objective pen of her closest friend: the author. (23)

The "author" (designated with the masculine French word *auteur* and named as a male friend, *un ami*) comments on the events in the third person; and the first-person narrator (N.) shares her personal account of love and loss in retelling her love affair with M. after it has ended. For the purposes of this essay, I attempt to delineate the depiction of N. as distinct from Barney herself, but the insistent slippage between the two makes this challenging. As the reader can see from the above quotation, Barney deliberately compels the reader to question any neat separation between N., the narrator, the fictional author, and Barney herself. Barney purposefully evokes the question of gender here as well, calling herself *un ami* (male friend), which is lost in translation: "her closest friend." In fact, the shifts that occur in the novel are numerous: first to third person, masculine to feminine, autobiography to fiction.

The philosophical chapter that introduces the character of N. sets up the blurring of autobiography and fiction from the beginning of the novel: "But to reassure you about N.—this third one who is anything but fictional—you must know that in every other respect, she is definitely human" (17). It also introduces the key concept of *la troisième* (which appears in the title of the work, *Amants féminins, ou, La troisième*); I translate this as the "third woman/lover/one," depending on the context. Oddly enough, a version of this chapter, titled "Portrait of the Author by the Author in Lieu of a Preface," opens *Traits et Portraits* (1963). It is unclear how this stand-alone philosophical musing on the category of the "third one" would have been received, especially without the accompanying narrative of the novel. Yet perhaps Barney felt that this section did not need the novel's context to be understood. The reason why Barney did not publish the full text of *Women Lovers, or The Third Woman* in her lifetime may never be known.

When a work is autobiographical, the pressure for "accuracy" in the translation is perhaps even greater, as the lexical choices can affect how particular historical personalities—not just characters—are seen. As noted in the epigraph above, Barney herself blurs the line between life and art in this playful pensée: "Works of art are sustained by betrayals in love. After the art of the flesh, works of art."[10] In fact, the writings of women who knew and loved Barney are so rich because love relationships and friendships lived off the page were—literally—the stuff of novels, and these relationships were "translated" into their writings: "The lines between the socio-political, the literary, and the erotic were blurred, as social relationships that were developed in the literary arena carried over into the personal one and vice versa. . . . Testing their (collective) ability to influence public discourse, the writers in Barney's circle engaged in a kind of *intertextual ideological collaboration.*"[11] Just as Melanie Hawthorne aptly notes in the introduction that *Women Lovers* can be seen as a kind of collage, melding conventional narrative with "poems, letters, social announcements (*faire-parts*), extracts from diaries, and dialogues to create an impression of a narrative assembled from fragments," so too does the literary output within this circle become a kind of collage. Making *Women Lovers* available for the first time in English adds one more piece to the puzzle. We benefit from the reading of these texts against one another, as they inform us and broaden our viewpoint.[12]

The "collage" effect of the novel, with the "realia" of (ostensibly) unedited letters placed directly in the manuscript, only serves to reinforce the impression that the novel itself is "raw writing," not written for readers' consumption.[13] Barney thus plays on readers' expectations of autobiographical writing, at once appearing "sincere" and at the same time consistently calling the readers' attention to the fact that all writing of the self is a performance. This novel, then, can be considered a precursor to the development of *autofiction*, a form developed in France in the 1970s "at a time of severely diminished faith in the power of memory or language to access definitive truths about the past or the self."[14] This roman à clef seeks to sabotage its status as such much earlier in literary history, and Barney constantly and deliberately blurs the line between autobiography and fiction, undermining the idea that objective writing is possible: "The scenes and commentary in the third person come from the objective pen of her closest friend: the author." The movement between the first- and third-person narrators emphasizes this constant tension throughout the text and calls into question the conventional wisdom that writing in the third person is more "objective" than first-person narration.

In order to make the biographical connections more transparent, I have provided a key in the form of a partial list of "dramatis personae" to help connect the characters in the novel with their real-life counterparts. Another example of a roman à clef from the same circle is *Ladies Almanack* by Djuna Barnes (1928), which overlaps with *Women Lovers* by including references to Mimi Franchetti, Natalie Barney, Liane de Pougy, Elisabeth de Gramont, and Romaine Brooks. The interlocutor (named N.M., for *La nouvelle malheureuse*) who emerges in the final dialogues of *Women Lovers* is none other than Djuna Barnes.[15] I translate *La nouvelle malheureuse* as "Newly Miserable One" (in part to retain the initials N.M., as in the French, because initials are so significant in this novel).

Another example of the rich intertextuality of the period is de Pougy's *journal intime*, *My Blue Notebooks*, in which de Pougy recounts her version of several key events that also appear in *Women Lovers*. The two works overlap in the telling of a pivotal event: de Pougy's husband, Prince Georges Ghika, leaves her after sixteen years of marriage for Manon Thiébaut (nicknamed "Tiny One"), who was living with them at the time and adored by both de Pougy and the Prince. In order to console her long-time friend, Barney introduces de Pougy to Barney's new lover, the Italian Mimi Franchetti. When Franchetti (who appears thinly veiled in the novel under the initial M.) and de Pougy (L.) fall in love, they exclude Barney and the love triangle falls apart. De Pougy depicts her subsequent love affair with Franchetti from her perspective in *My Blue Notebooks*:

> [Nathalie and Mimy] made much of me, they took me out, they dressed my wounds. Mimy and I loved each other. Her presence was my heaven of joy and forgetfulness.

Nathalie became jealous. Nathalie loves in her own way. She wants her friends to be happy up to a certain point. She is dissolute; she adores directing love's revels, leading them on, halting them, starting them up again. What she loves is bodies, and reactions.[16]

In contrast to de Pougy's version, *Women Lovers* foregrounds Barney's view that her renewed erotic entanglement with de Pougy was born out of selfless motives: N. describes her creation of an "association" with M., whose goal is to "come [to] the aid" of women who are in distress, who are "tormented or hurt." Addressing M., N. outlines the goals of this "association":

Since we love women, don't we have a duty to their sorrow and their abandonment?

We won't judge others against ourselves, and we won't compare ourselves to them either. As specialists who aren't summoned unless the situation truly calls for it, we should leave once the patient, the *love-sick*, no longer needs special care, when just anyone can continue the treatment and take over.[17] (38)

Whereas N. creates an intricate theoretically or philosophically based "association" as justification for introducing her then-lover M. to L., de Pougy references none of that in her journal: she simply delights in being taken care of by N.: "She held me in her arms, listened, advised, sent flowers, took me to the Duchess', showed me the sweetest and most compassionate tenderness."[18] The reader may surmise that—not surprisingly— L. was apparently never told about these loftier, idealistic goals of an "association." Perhaps, too, Barney herself trumped up her motives after the fact, by foregrounding this philosophical framework when writing the novel; this would only serve to make the betrayal of Barney by de Pougy all the greater in the reader's eyes, as N.'s decision to introduce M. to L. results in such emotional disarray, at least for N. Her motives, in other words, appear in many ways to be selfless.

This is not to say that Barney's main aim in writing the book is to flatter herself. One of the most disarming aspects of the novel, one could

argue, is the way in which the narrator attempts to look critically at herself. "The Newly Miserable One" (N.M., aligned with Djuna Barnes)
encourages N. to write a novel that moves beyond the "mask":

> Do you have any doubt? Don't make yourself out to be better
> than you are: tender, deceived, melting. Reveal your diabolical
> side, throw out your demons: they are suffocating you. Love as
> you write: with cynicism, with science. Why hide behind this faint
> and feigned docility that is your—mask . . . (159)

The goal of this work, then, is for N. to "reveal [her] diabolical side"
and "not make [herself] to be better than [she is]." N. leaves the impression that she follows this advice, with telling revelations that represent
a kind of self-examination: "And even if I had M. to myself, would I
be satisfied, like L. is?" (125). In a self-critical gesture, she admits that she
may not be satisfied, even if she had what she thinks that she wants! This
key phrase poignantly foregrounds the erotic and relational tension in
the novel; she wants what she does not have: "When I am alone with
someone, I think of those that I am not with" (125). Part of the ironic
subtext of the novel is that, while N. feels betrayed and becomes madly
jealous when M. falls in love with L., Barney has two (what might be
called) primary love relationships ongoing in her life, with Elisabeth de
Gramont and painter Romaine Brooks.[19] Due to circumstances outside
of Barney's control, both de Gramont and Brooks are unavailable to her
at the time of the breakup with M., making the sting of rejection and
loss even more painful. In this light, however, N.'s hostility toward L.,
evident throughout the novel, could be viewed as hypocritical in many
ways: Barney continually had brief love affairs throughout these two relationships with de Gramont and Brooks (that overlapped in her life for
many years). As Melanie Hawthorne writes in the introduction, "Barney
once offered a list of her primary relationships, divided into *liaisons* (serious relationships), *demi-liaisons* (semi-serious affairs), and *aventures* (flings).
The relationship with Pougy counted as a serious affair, but Mimi Franchetti is mentioned only as an *aventure*."

In the translation, the emotional ties between the women must be rendered as clearly as possible, necessitating substantive choices affecting how
each relationship is understood. For readability's sake, I have uniformly
formatted how Romaine Brooks and Elisabeth de Gramont are named
throughout the novel. *L'amie-la-plus-chère* is translated consistently as "Dearest Friend" and quite pointedly refers to Romaine Brooks; her letters are
signed R. The designation for Elisabeth de Gramont is more complicated,
as the tense changes periodically, moving from *La femme-que-N.-avait-le-plus-
aimée* (which could be translated as "The Woman N. *Had* Loved the Most,"
emphasis mine) to *La femme-que-j'ai-le-plus-aimée* (which could be translated
as "The Woman I Loved the Most"). Given the strength of the relationship between the two women (culminating in a symbolic marriage contract in 1918 to assuage de Gramont's jealousy of Romaine Brooks[20]), I
translated it as "The Woman I Loved the Most" to convey more of a
sense of immediacy. Another example of how the translator must parse
issues of emotional volatility is the interpretation of the phrasing *une
nouvelle emotion.* When M. leaves with L., N. doesn't emphasize to the reader
the ironic fact that she is alone *only* because Romaine Brooks is not able to
meet her as planned. Brooks's reason? She has *une nouvelle emotion* (literally
"has a new emotion"), which I translate as "being emotionally involved,"
preserving the idea of emotion and leaving the extent of the engagement
ambiguous, as in the French, rather than using more explicit wording
such as having "a new thrill" or, even stronger, "a new love interest."

Translating the key term *la troisième* proved formidable as well. As noted
above, gender is a central issue in the novel, and I have written elsewhere
about the gendered dynamics of lovemaking and self-identity in the
novel.[21] Though, according to Jean Chalon, Barney never would have
called herself a *féministe*, issues of gender were central to Barney's work,
as the title of one section of her groundbreaking oeuvre, *Pensées d'une
Amazone*, attests: "Les Sexes Adverses" (with a subcategory being "La
Guerre et le Féminisme").[22] Moving from the role of scholar to that of
translator, however, made me wary to overemphasize the issue of gender in
the translation. In the more philosophical, theoretical sections on *la troisième*
as its own category, for example, I elected to use the term "third one" to

allow for a more open-ended reading. In context of a particular situation in the plot, however, I normally translated it as "third woman" or "third lover." On one occasion, I took the liberty of translating using the English expression "third wheel," which worked well in the context of the plot.

The issue becomes even more complex in passages where Barney moves between the terms *le troisième* and *la troisième*. In one case, I initially interpreted this movement between the masculine and the feminine terms as perhaps echoing the broader eroticized gender play in the novel; in fact, their use was simply grammatical (when *le troisième* simply refers back to the masculine word *le personnage*). In another instance, however, it appears that Barney uses *le troisième* and *la troisième* interchangeably:

> They are three equals, but can there be equal parts? Would the third woman [*la troisième*] have the best part of it?
>   In order to be third [*le troisième*], you need to be the strongest of the three. You must be all three, all that the third one [*le troisième*] encompasses. (88)

This one is so puzzling it makes one wonder if there is some kind of error here. As the reader can see in the translated example above, I made the stylistic and thematic choice to not always invoke the gender of the term. In other instances, I decided to use the context of the love affair between the three women to inform my choice, changing "he" in the French to "she" in the translation, as in this passage: "Exposed and re-wounded again and again in her vulnerability, *she* finds its raison d'être—and is forgiven for *her* wounds that sing" (89, emphasis mine).[23]

Finally, the key term found in the title—*amant féminin*—was perhaps the most difficult to translate, as it appears to juxtapose the idea of a masculine lover—*amant*—with the adjective *féminin*. At first, I translated the title as *Feminine Lovers, or The Third Woman*, to emphasize the issue of gender. The history of the word *amant* reveals that the feminine form—*amante*—was in use only from the twelfth to the seventeenth century.[24] So, for the time period in which Barney was writing, *amant* would have been the word of choice. This does not settle the question entirely, however. Even if the word *amant* might be considered a gender-neutral word

in twentieth-century French, Barney still appears to be deliberately point-
ing to the issue of gender in the title, with the adjective *féminins*. In the
end, however, I felt that the book itself treats the issue of gender, without needing to overemphasize it in the title. Once I became clearer on the
use of *amant*, I modified my translation of the following line: "C'est en
amant que je jugerais mon amant," which at first I translated as "It is the
man in me that will judge the man in her." Although this translation does
convey a sense of tension in the scene (which further down the page jux-
taposes the term *amant* with *maîtresse*), I felt that it would be too distracting
in the English and call *too* much attention to the issue of gender. I wound
up translating it as "In any case, it is as a lover that I will judge her as a
lover" (37). In a previous passage she underscores the idea that both N.
and M. can play both roles: "But the mistress would be less inclined to
cheat on me than the lover, and my feminine pride defends me against
the latter" (36). As the reader may surmise, the novel is replete with
paradoxes concerning gender and sexual identity; the fact that French has
gendered nouns does not make the process of translating the novel into
English any easier. I hope that this translator's essay highlights the com-
plexity to the reader, while leaving the issue open to fresh interpretation.

In many ways, this novel is one of Barney's best pieces of writing—
the lyrical qualities of her pensées translated into novel form.[25] The most
compelling passages are perhaps those on loving and loss, written by the
woman for whom "living in the present moment ... was her greatest
strength."[26]

I miss everything I did not have. I miss everything I did have. And
everything I shall have no longer? And this life, too alive, that we
shall have to bury. . . . [. . .]
But why have regrets if I can find it again, imagine it, feel it
once more? What good is having lived this with you if I cannot
revive you? (103)

The novel left to the archives is now before you in translation, bringing the vibrant characters of Paris 1926 to life once again in this modern
novel, revived for us to appreciate, through Barney's singular voice.

NOTES

1. Nathalie Fressard, pers. comm., September 2013. Fressard is a librarian at the Bibliothèque Littéraire Jacques Doucet in Paris. She confirmed that Barney's will, written on December 12, 1968, gave all of her unpublished manuscripts and correspondence at her home the day of her death to the library. The archives were transferred after her death in 1972, and in 1977 they were accepted by the Chancellerie des Universités de Paris. François Chapon was already the director of the library, having started in 1957, and he became executor of Barney's works upon her death. In speaking with biographer Jean Chalon about her choice of the Bibliothèque Littéraire Jacques Doucet, Chapon said that it was a great honor and Barney was flattered to have her materials there. Jean Chalon, pers. comm., September 2013. See note 3 for additional information on Chalon.

2. Suzanne Rodriguez, *Wild Heart: A Life: Natalie Clifford Barney's Journey from Victorian America to the Literary Salons of Paris* (New York: HarperCollins, 2002), 277. Rodriguez provides a number of short quotations from the novel; I consulted them when translating those passages and am indebted to her work.

3. Jean Chalon, pers. comm., September 2013. Biographer of Barney, Liane de Pougy, and others, Chalon has published numerous works on the period, including *Chère Natalie Barney* (Paris: Stock, 1976) and *Liane de Pougy: Courtisane, princesse, sainte* (Paris: Flammarion, 1994). He is also the last living person who was close to Barney.

4. For a discussion of the influence of Baudelaire on this novel, see Chelsea Ray, "Decadent Heroines or Modernist Lovers: Natalie Clifford Barney's Unpublished *Feminine Lovers or the Third Woman*," *South Central Review* 22, no. 3 (2005): 32–61. Barney's other modernist novel, *The One Who Is Legion, or A.D. Afterlife* (1930, published in English), underscores her interest in literary experimentation in the period between the two world wars.

5. Natalie Clifford Barney, *Amants féminins, ou, La troisième*, ed. Chelsea Ray and Yvan Quintin (Aurillac: ErosOnyx Éditions, 2013). The French edition both facilitated my work and posed a special translation problem, as I had begun working on the translation prior to the French publication and my translation of the novel had been based on the manuscript rather than on the final, edited version. Because of this, the reader may find slight variations between the published French version and the translation, as I have sometimes made choices that differ a bit from the French version in keeping with the original manuscript. Both the French and English editions eliminated many of Barney's ellipses, as they were excessive and distracting. One of the challenges of working with Barney's unpublished manuscript was that some of the chapter titles in her table of contents do not appear in the body of the novel. In this translation, we made the decision to include a few of these chapter titles (some of which do not appear in the French edition) because they add meaning to the content, and the brevity of the chapters underscores the quick tempo of this modernist work. For the original table of contents, see Barney, *Amants féminins*, 170–71.

6. Suzanne Rodriguez's biography provides information on Barney learning French at a young age. Rodriguez, *Wild Heart*, 35–36, 40–41. For additional biographical information on Barney, see Diana Souhami, *Wild Girls: Paris, Sappho, and Art: The Lives and Loves of Natalie Clifford Barney and Romaine Brooks* (New York: St. Martin's Press, 2004).

7. Natalie Clifford Barney, *Quelques portraits-sonnets de femmes* (Verona: L'Amazone Retrouvée, 1999), vii (my translation).

8. Alice Kaplan, "Translation: The Biography of An Art Form," in *Translation: Translators on Their Work and What It Means*, ed. Esther Allen and Susan Bernofsky, 67–81 (New York: Columbia University Press, 2013), 72.

9. For information about the two sections of the novel that have been published, see note 10 on page 16.

10. Natalie Clifford Barney, *Pensées d'une Amazone* (Paris: Émile-Paul, 1920), 101, my translation.

11. Chelsea Ray, "Mythology and Ideology: Literary Depictions of Natalie Clifford Barney in *L'Ange et les pervers*, *Ladies Almanack*, and *Amants féminins ou la troisième*," *Women in French Studies* (Special Issue, 2010): 91–92.

12. The list of works that include Barney is impressive: "It should come as no surprise that writers who knew and loved Barney depicted her in their fictional works. Life-as-art, then, comes full circle, as Barney's life is refracted back through literary portraits. She appears as Flossie in Liane de Pougy's *Idylle saphique* (1901), Miss Flossie in Colette's *Claudine s'en va* (1903), Vally and Lorély in Renée Vivien's *Une femme m'apparut* (1904, rewritten in 1905), Valerie Seymour in Radclyffe Hall's *The Well of Loneliness* (1928), Dame Evangeline Musset in Djuna Barnes's *Ladies Almanack* (1928), and Laurette Wells in Lucie Delarue-Mardrus's *L'Ange et les pervers* (1930)." Ray, "Mythology and Ideology," 91. It is important, however, not to fall into the trap of believing that these works are a "true-to-life" representation of Barney. For further discussion, see Melanie Hawthorne's discussion in the introduction on the relationship between the initials and the women.

13. Biographer Jean Chalon confirmed these are actual letters that were not edited for the novel. Jean Chalon, pers. comm., January 2016.

14. "Autofiction," in *Encyclopedia of Life Writing: Autobiographical and Biographical Forms* (London: Routledge, 2001).

15. From his personal conversations with Barney on the love affair with Mimi, Jean Chalon was able to confirm without a doubt that N.M. is indeed Djuna Barnes. Jean Chalon, pers. comm., September 2013.

16. Liane de Pougy, *My Blue Notebooks*, trans. Diana Athill (New York: Putnam, 2002), 203 (spelling of names retained from original work). De Pougy discusses her relationship with Franchetti on pages 201–14. In addition, de Pougy and Barney co-wrote a chapter in de Pougy's novel *Idylle saphique* (Paris: Jean-Claude Lattès, 1979) detailing their relationship.

17. It is interesting to note that both de Pougy and Barney use medical metaphors to describe the support offered in the beginning; as noted earlier, de Pougy characterizes it as "dress[ing] [her] wounds," and Barney symbolically refers to de Pougy as the patient who is "*love-sick*." The italics in the translation indicate where a word was originally written in English.

18. De Pougy, *My Blue Notebooks*, 202. Interestingly, Suzanne Rodriguez does not emphasize the theoretical and conceptual aspect of this renewed relationship (through the idea of the "association"), instead calling these "caretaking visits" whose aim it was to "divert." Rodriguez, *Wild Heart*, 277, 278.

19. The real-life complexities of all these relationships are stunning—Mimi Franchetti had an affair with Elisabeth de Gramont in 1924 and Romaine Brooks and Mimi Franchetti had an affair in the spring of 1925, right before the events of this novel. In addition, Liane de Pougy and Elisabeth de Gramont were briefly together! According to biographer Rapazzini, rumor had it that Brooks and de Gramont may also have had an affair. For additional information, see Richard Davenport-Hines, *Proust at the Majestic: The Last Days of the Author Whose Book Changed Paris* (New York: Bloomsbury Publishing, 2006), 24, and Francesco Rapazzini, *Elisabeth de Gramont: Avant-gardiste* (Paris: Librarie Arthème Fayard, 2004). Suzanne Stroh's English translation of this biography is forthcoming. For the most recent biography on Brooks, see Cassandra Langer, *Romaine Brooks: A Life* (Madison: University of Wisconsin Press, 2015). In addition to discussing Brooks's relationship with Franchetti (111), Langer provides new information about the end of Natalie and Romaine's relationship and the grief that Barney experienced at the loss of her lifetime love (194–97). Barney was ninety-three and Brooks ninety-four when this final split occurred.

20. Rapazzini, *Elisabeth de Gramont*, 336–37. For the full text of this marriage contract, see 340–42.

21. Ray, "Decadent Heroines or Modernist Lovers."

22. Barney, *Pensées d'une Amazone*, 1. In a recent conversation with Jean Chalon, he stated that, like Colette, these were women who were claimed by later feminists as their own, but they did not necessarily see themselves as feminist. He hinted that they may have seen this as imitating men, which they felt no need to do. Jean Chalon, pers. comm., September 2013.

23. Here is the quotation in the French edition: "À vif et reblessé sans cesse dans sa vulnérabilité, il y trouve sa raison d'être—et se fait pardonner ses blessures qui chantent" (92).

24. "Amant/e," in *Dictionnaire de l'Académie française, neuvième* édition: *Version informatisée.*

25. To learn more about Barney's pensées, see Chelsea Ray, "Sexual Politics in Early French Feminism: Natalie Clifford Barney's *Pensées d'une Amazone,*" in *Cherchez la Femme: Women and Values in the Francophone World,* ed. Erika Fulop and Adrienne Angelo, 27–38 (Cambridge: Cambridge Scholars, 2011).

26. Jean Chalon, pers. comm., September 2013.

Dramatis Personae

This list includes all the characters whose "real life" identity is clear.

L. = Liane de Pougy
M. = Mimi de Franchetti
N. = Natalie Clifford Barney
N.M., or the Newly Miserable Woman = Djuna Barnes
R., or Dearest Friend = Romaine Brooks
Woman N. Loved the Most = Elisabeth de Gramont
T. = Thelma Woods

Women Lovers, or
The Third Woman

Written around 1926
for
MIMI FRANCHETTI
N.C.B.[1]

---

1. This handwritten notation appears on the first page of the manuscript in Barney's hand.

Table of Contents

3

Tonight . . .

Tonight Sappho sleeps in dreams with Cyprus . . .[2]
I give myself to your shadow, and in your name arrives
My body's extraordinary pleasure, untouched by men
—You are the only one who took my own body from me!

I will take away my joy from these mouths, though they
Barely know how to entertain my sensuality.
Offered to the memory of your brutality
I refuse to give myself over, even to my most beautiful slave.

Dear feminine Phaon, let everything be taken from me
—Satisfy unfulfilled women with your love—
I tilt back my head under your absent face

---

2. In her early writing, Barney regularly drew upon Greek tropes in order to present (and perhaps validate) her vision of lesbian love. She idealized Sappho's school of poetry, even traveling to Lesbos with Renée Vivien with the plan of creating a school of women poets. In 1927, she created the Academy of Women as a feminist response to the conservative all-male Académie française, modeled on Sappho's school of poetry. For more information, see Joan DeJean, *Fictions of Sappho (1546–1937)* (Chicago: University of Chicago Press, 1989). Karla Jay's groundbreaking study also provides important context. Karla Jay, *The Amazon and the Page: Natalie Clifford Barney and Renée Vivien* (Bloomington: Indiana University Press, 1988).

Taken by your complete beauty, I'm everything they can
 never be.

Without submitting to your mouth's disdain that curves toward
Your passenger, the unfaithful smuggler
I am the only one who completely possesses my possessor
I am the one who knows—the heights we fall from in her small
 boat.

Waiting, waiting in vain for your fervor, disappointed
By an absurd rival; being jealous, I am silent.
Needing another being is a kind of adultery,
That counters the majesty hidden in Oneself.

I will never again dance this amorous dance
Of the couple, threatened by the most acute grief—
Putting our voluptuousness beyond our pride.
Does human dependency enrich us or debase us?

In spite of you, far from you, my desire is fulfilled
Truer than the truths of your ecstatic women,
Like a lover, deprived of her beloved's face,
Tonight your likeness visited my bed.

And I violated the contours of your sleeping body,
Laid out in the subconscious, a reflection of reality,
And out of the strange union of our completed being
I created a new species of dreams, in your image.[3]

N.C.B.

---

3. This image echoes a more elaborated theme in Barney's *Pensées d'une Amazone*, where she references *"this visionary and miraculous childbirth of dreams that are longer lasting and perhaps more alike than earthly generations"* (emphasis in original, my translation). This idea of "childbirth of dreams" takes inspiration from Diotima's speech at the end of Plato's *Symposium*, which privileges spiritual over physical begetting. Barney, *Pensées d'une Amazone* (Paris: Émile-Paul, 1920; repr. with critical commentary, 1921), 113.

Portraits of Three Women

I

Portrait of L.

The great courtesan, the little saint.

"Sacred and profane love," whether naked or dressed—just as in Titian's painting—they look more alike than sisters![4] They are the same.

Either she hoards, or she's full of renunciation. Just as emotional in sacrifice as in selfishness.

Incapable of abstraction, pious as a maid, but with a few remaining traces of nobler origins, she takes matters in hand and responds like a master in important situations. But at other times she lets go and thrusts her beautiful, greedy, and well-nourished mouth toward all carnal pleasures. Her hands are heavy and latch on to things, her fingers are folded inward, as if to avoid praying.

Her eyes scrutinize, but see nothing as a whole. Her eyes say: "I want that too." Either too close or too far away, she sees nothing but a silhouette.

Simple like a book block print, her brain only understands the obvious.

She lets herself be carried along by circumstances: accustomed to a horizontal position, she floats on her back, and it is in seeing herself that she becomes conscious of herself and others.

---

4. Barney here provocatively references Titian's painting *Sacred and Profane Love* (c. 1514) in order to depict metaphorically these two sides of Liane de Pougy. The painting features two female figures, one dressed and one semi-nude, with a winged infant appearing in the middle.

She is concerned with herself and nothing else.

Scatological in her words—very "earthy"—with sudden bursts of purity. Despite her years in the love trade, something honest and healthy—like her thin-lipped, curved, and sensual mouth—emanates from her whole body, a body so well preserved that she looks like a primitive half-virgin with clumsy feet, feet that give her a dignified carriage, but prevent her from dancing.

Thoughtless, childlike, and spoiled, most of her personality seems to have remained in childhood. Touchy when it comes to herself, yet insensitive to others, she is never so much at ease as when she doesn't belong.

In a salon her naked hands move languorously from shoulder to shoulder—waiting to pounce decisively upon her prey.

Appearing kind on the surface, she takes small things to heart, such as making a fuss over a manicure, yet remains intractable and cold when it comes to serious trouble. Professing gratitude, she has a complete change of heart when faced with the slightest criticism, having fragile nerves and an unforgiving heart (and it's better not to be at the mercy of either of them).

A lingering voice that latches onto you like perfume, the voice of an 1890s boudoir.

The sentimentality of a young girl taking her first communion—which serves her interests well. She has the skillful inquisitiveness of a priest and the chastity of a font of holy water polished by everyone's touch.

None of it has left any trace except for the tiny superficial lines etched in the shimmering oval of her face . . .

Pretty as a heart—a heart with no expression—even her handwriting says it.

She normalizes desire, and in the end, she domesticates you better than any wife would. She reserves you for her exclusive service and reduces you to slavery, without worrying about what would ever cross a slave's mind.

That's why she was more surprised than hurt when her husband asserted his authority one day by taking up with a young mistress and then running off with her.

For years she had leaned on him in public like a cane—a cane she didn't need. He looked like a swamp just asking to be stirred up. His poor little back—that of a four-thousand-year-old adolescent fossil—seemed petrified in this pose of pointless devotion. His bowed posture made it look like he was always looking for something to do for her: "What do you want, my love?" Perhaps he subconsciously knew her answer: "I want to be bored without you—I want to be bored in some other way!" And wasn't it the last act of a good husband to rid her of himself and their oppressive happiness, which had become suffocating and more demoralizing than prostitution?

After the surgical shock of the separation, and a few nights of insomnia, L. pursued her simple destiny, as in *The Songs of Bilitis*, the somewhat jumbled songs of Bilitis:

> A courtesan in youth
> A married woman in middle age
> A lesbian in old age . . .[5]

And "God's mistress" in the end?

------

5. In 1894, Pierre Louÿs published *Chansons de Bilitis*, a literary coup that became even more famous after it was revealed to be a hoax. While the text purported to be a carefully researched translation of poetry by Bilitis, a contemporary of Sappho, it was later revealed to be written by Louÿs himself. It should be noted that these three lines are not directly quoted from this work. Louÿs's *Chansons de Bilitis* appealed to Barney because it presented Classical Greece "as a liberating alternative to the petit-bourgeois values of the present age." Jay, *The Amazon and the Page*, 62. For further information on the literary friendship between Louÿs and Barney, see Suzanne Rodriguez, *Wild Heart: A Life: Natalie Clifford Barney's Journey from Victorian America to the Literary Salons of Paris* (New York: HarperCollins, 2002) 131–34, 138.

II

Portrait of M.

To M.[6]

She is thirty-three years old, when everyone else is older.
The pallor of the tribes of Israel brightens her face,
She has drunk from the cup discarded by Christ.

Every day puts a cross on her proud shoulders
Which do not bend like the Son of God's back,
Whose misery was told around the world.

Since her stoical spirit and her Adonis-like appearance
Know how to face the offense, the crucifixion and the sponge,
And love's life—all are our bad dreams.

See you tonight—my true little companion, my dear twin.[7]

~

---

6. "This handwritten poem appears on the back of page 3 of the manuscript. The second verse does not rhyme. Someone (who?) put the word *tribus* after the word *visage*, which does not make sense here. The reader may note a number of grammatical or metrical oddities." Natalie Clifford Barney, *Amants féminins, ou, La troisième*, ed. Chelsea Ray and Yvan Quintin (Aurillac: ErosOnyx Éditions, 2013), 32n20. Notes translated from the French edition are labeled as such. Some notes were modified or excluded when content was not relevant for an English-speaking audience.

7. This line underscores the importance of Baudelaire to Barney, as it echoes the end of his famous poem "To the Reader" in *Flowers of Evil* (1857) by referring to M. as *mon cher semblable*, which I translate as "my dear twin." The translation loses

M.'s defining characteristics:
  She has had more than one hundred mistresses.
  She ignores dramas and letters.
  She scaled the face of B. _____.[8]
  She is thirty-three years old, when everyone else is older.

She slits her wrists over the slightest upset, but dreads going to the dentist and coming home to her apartment alone at night.

She has universal appeal, but can't keep anyone. You quickly fall under her spell, but the charm is short-lived and doesn't work from afar.

Failing to be the perfect mother for a child she couldn't have, she is the dreamed-of lover for women who dream and who are not afraid of waking up!

Her snooping at the window has made her nose grow a bit longer; she's up to date, and yet her hair is a bit too short to be fashionable. She was more seductive when she had curls.

She is wan like the children of Israel who still pale at the thought of having crucified their God.

Her fire is exceptional and endowed with every trick.

---

the gender play in the novel, as *mon cher semblable* is in the masculine. I discuss my treatment of gender issues in the translator's essay. French biographer Jean Chalon asserted that Baudelaire was indeed an exceptional literary influence in Barney's life, calling him "the preferred poet of Natalie." Characterizing himself and Barney as "two devotees of Baudelaire," Chalon recounted how Barney would often ask him to recite Baudelaire's three poems on lesbian love, which Chalon knew by heart. Jean Chalon, pers. comm., March 2005. For a discussion of the influence of Baudelaire on *Women Lovers*, see Chelsea Ray, "Decadent Heroines or Modernist Lovers: Natalie Clifford Barney's Unpublished *Feminine Lovers or the Third Woman*," *South Central Review* 22, no. 3 (2005): 32–61.

8. "This capital letter has undecipherable writing after it that was added. Perhaps it is Brévet, the name of a mountain peak in the Alps." Barney, *Amants féminins*, 33n21. Another possible mountain could be Boespitze in the Dolomites, today known as Piz Boè, which towers over the Gardena Valley. Mimi's brother Carlo, the explorer Baron Raimondo Franchetti (1889–1935), bought the seventeenth-century Schloss Gröden in the Gardena Valley in 1926, the same year that *Women Lovers* was written. The Franchettis still own Schloss Gröden today. Suzanne Stroh, pers. comm., August 2013.

She says: "It is awful to be taken, it is appalling to take." But that's all she does!

When not doing that, she sings.

She knows all the great operas and foxtrots by heart—including the words!

And entire *cantos* by Dante—and Paul Géraldy![9]

She reads more than she sleeps.

She has a fine memory, but does not always remember the best part.

She is more passionate than sensual, which often leads her to be wrong—something she readily admits. Where others refuse to let go, she moves on. Her choice is rushed, depending on the moment, the setting, and on two double *kummel* liqueurs.

In summer, she usually swears off drinking, and it only takes her two days out in the countryside to get a tan.

She is skilled in anything and everything—but never practices. She avoids unnecessary gestures, except flicking her lighter to cigarettes, one after the other.

She is careful, never sets fire to her sheets, rarely burns holes in her clothes, which she wears well and with care—until the moment she puts them away.

She prefers her handkerchiefs to her perfume.

Her toiletry case is orderly and well kept—as if she had just received it for her birthday. She puts each object back in its place—and returns wives to their husbands, after taking advantage of them.

Husbands woo her during this auspicious time. They've got it backward!

She attracts men to whom she is not attracted; actually, she isn't attracted to any man . . . not even the manly woman. Only the womanly woman, the woman in her full bloom, the female woman—the feminine in all its forms, even if excessively so.

She is not hostile to the masculine gender and would have many male friends if they didn't ruin their chances by trying to become wretched

---

9. Paul Géraldy (1885–1983) was a poet and a playwright.

lovers, something she could stand only if she were blind drunk—and not even then! She almost never wears feminine clothing so as not to mislead them. She avoids cavorting in social circles for the same reason, especially since she doesn't always have a tart to inflict upon society!

All boredom needs to have a goal—and that is why she writes sometimes to her financial advisors as well as the men in her family.

She has a certain sense of solidarity—and would even have a sense of loyalty to her family—if her family had not been so discouraging.

Her instincts and intuition are flashes that do not afford her any real psychological insight. Her artistic temperament, having love as its sole occupation, is the reason for her idleness. Beneath the grandeur of a great lord, the lavish tips of a dubious foreign parvenu.

She has the naivety of a foreigner, which excuses her lack of taste and even her missteps in love, as they stem from a lack of awareness.

Her hands are more evolved than she herself is, and they get hurt on everything, just as souls do.

Her long hands are a blessing to behold—they are in exile close to the women they touch lightly or settle on, awaiting other paradises.

III

Portrait of N.

THE THIRD ONE, IN LIEU OF A PREFACE[10]

N. belongs to that category of people that may become less rare when the age-old earthly couple is definitively discredited, permitting each person to keep or rediscover her own wholeness.

At that point in human evolution, there will be no more "marriages," only ties based on tenderness and passion. Infinitely more delicate antennae will carry out the aerial game of relationships. These comings and goings will make some room—you must come from elsewhere to produce something new.

The end of faithfulness, that dead zone of unity, will be replaced by a perpetual becoming.

While awaiting the perfection of this total being, the "third ones" struggle between these two extremes: "Neither together, nor apart."

---

10. "A notably different version of this self-portrait (shorter in some sections and longer in others) was published in Barney, *Traits et Portraits* (Paris: Mercure de France, 1963; repr. 2002). It appears there under the title of 'Portrait of the author by the author in lieu of a preface.' Barney had already given a version of this text to Jean Royère, which he published in his journal *Le Manuscrit autographe*, no. 38 (1932): 96–98. This publication was modified in certain sections, and stopped four paragraphs before the end of the preface. The chapter entitled 'The Third Ones' was published in the same journal number (98–99), alongside the self-portrait." Barney, *Amants féminins*, 36n22. In the manuscript, the following was written by hand above the title: "Two chapters from an unpublished novel / Portrait of the Third Woman."

Unable to form part of a permanent couple, they still bear a very real sense of anguish in their intermediary, isolated state. They share enough traits with "those like themselves but who are not the same" to recognize themselves in them, but not enough to identify with them. It is not enough for them to lose themselves there and to stay there.

But to reassure you about N.—this third one who is anything but fictional—you must know that in every other respect, she is definitely human.

The couple will, however, remain her enemy—the couple she is a part of every bit as much as the one that excludes her—because isn't our enemy the one who is necessary to us and opposes us?

This odd-one-out—this unique one—works toward the destruction of the couple, just as the couple works toward the destruction of the odd-one-out.

This third woman is not looking for her other half or someone to complete her, but a twin—a "companion in love"—a variation of her kind that is infinitely variable—from the most confirmed homosexual to the angel—such wings!

While waiting for celestial pleasure, she wants a pleasure so similar that it could be mistaken as such. And, according to an author who wrote about a "triumphant invert" of our times, she communes with humans through joyful pleasure, even though she seems to miss out on it in every other way. She was made for this, made for these sovereign exaltations . . . Sometimes, this dream comes to fruition under exceptional circumstances, in a kind of rare fiery moment when ardor dissolves the "remains of our inadequacies."[11]

An Epicurean with overdeveloped senses, and blessed with the kind of joy that leads straight to martyrdom, she suffers in isolation with rage and patience.

---

11. While in the French publication there are quotation marks around this line starting with "she communes" (Barney, *Amants féminins*, 37), I follow the manuscript's use of quotation marks. It is unclear whether this is a direct quotation from the author who wrote about the "triumphant invert."

Constantly surprised, hurt, frustrated in the same way. Imaginative, trusting, and too willing to go along with others to watch out for her own best interests, she doesn't notice cunning and hidden motives. Sincere to the point of sadism, tender, sensitive, passionate yet modest, self-disciplined, and polite to the point of cowardice, no one has seen her suffer, no one has ever pitied her or come to her aid.

(Besides, anyone who came near her at such a moment would quickly receive an earful of sarcasm and the impression of cynicism rather than sorrow.

Her tears crystallize into diamonds of irony, scratching those who dare express pity. And wounds are only bearable with a smile.)

In any case, the third woman never stops to watch herself suffer. If there is a mirror, it is only for watching others.

Not one to spend much time on her appearance, she is surrounded by an uncomfortable chaos.

A buried voice that bubbles up to the surface, quivering with authority or deep with affection. A weak heart—yet tenacious. Harshness you'd never expect. Uncompromising nerves of steel. Sociable yet impossible to live with. Fawning over strangers, yet brutal with those closest to her. A good enough opinion of herself to do without flattery. Laziness overtakes her thirst and longing for fame. Almost nothing and no one is sacred to her. She tramples the tactless, and this harsh treatment (as if from a slave owner) makes them all the more tactless.

Lacking firm convictions, her point of view depends on what is in front of her. She values honesty, not so much for its intrinsic value, but more like a rule of the game. Flexible and sophisticated, she has as much contempt for justice as for those who practice it professionally. Her judgment is a sign of vengeance. She enjoys dominating and quickly tires of those she dominates. The temperament of a predator without seeking to take advantage of her prey. Many think her stingy, taking as avarice her ability to manage her own affairs—as well as those of others—so that she can put them out of her mind. They come to her in need, yet consider her shrewd. She spends her ingenuity rather than her money—which increases them both!

Her remaining traits are like something out of a fortune cookie, as they would appear on one of those bits of bright green, blue, or yellow paper that you used to get from the beggar's parrot in the Tuileries gardens. We notice not our similarity to others, but rather what makes us different. It is useless to list the ways in which this third woman can be as unfair, jealous, and petty as anyone. Selfless and with no ulterior motive— then fearful and distrustful of everything—except of what was bound to happen. Her intelligence only works with precision in the abstract and does not work efficiently for human interactions, where good faith is the worst kind of faith—because when everyone cheats, it becomes dishonest to play fair.

Sharpened all the same by the defeats that her conquests earned her, she nonetheless sets her sights on another ideal that is just as out of reach.

Her quick and churning mind does not allow for contingencies—is it because what was supposed to happen never does? There is no stopping her mind's activity, because it operates in some imaginary realm, only stopping when the tiniest bit of reality finally derails it.

After this often empty burst of enthusiasm, her heart beating when it shouldn't, her mind sifts through what she has lived in slow motion, and lingers after the fruit in the orchard is gone.

An exceptional being in a mundane world, she has a mind that clashes with the actions of others, a protagonist in a novel that never seems to be her own.

When the third woman covets another being, it is only a matter of time before this being—stirred by this sense of comforting well-being— decides sooner or later to search for her other half and a home elsewhere, eventually becoming suspicious and rejecting the third woman as an unknown "outlier," as the Normans call someone who only pretends to want to stay among them.[12]

---

12. The idea of searching for one's other half is a reference to Plato's *Symposium*, in which there are three sexes: male, female, and androgynous. Split into two, they search for their other half. Melanie Hawthorne's introduction to the translation provides a reading of this as it pertains specifically to the "third one" in this novel. There is also a play on words here; the term *hors sein* (meaning "outside the

They sense that this third one is not one of their own:

I never was attached to that great sect,
Whose doctrine is, that each one should select
Out of the crowd a mistress or a friend,
And all the rest, though fair and wise, condemn
To cold oblivion.[13]

This third one, this unique misfit, this one-off, this isolated, mis-matched, odd-one-out among the coupled, is locked out and usually presented as a Seducer, rather than a victim of her unattached state. By nature rather than by choice, she is forced to differentiate herself from others without being able to free herself from them.

And doesn't she owe to her intimate connections—which are nothing more than brief instants of joy, harmony, and distraction—a whole life spent in isolation, where she atones in solitude for her carnal appetites?

If these portraits don't turn out or are not true to life, if they "don't do justice," blame the author, who will in turn blame the state of mind she was reduced to when bringing them out of the inner shadows into the light of day.

The precipitate of the events faithfully recorded here will perhaps illustrate them better; it is up to readers to evaluate for themselves these raw materials—thrown together in no particular order—and to take the side of the character they find the least disagreeable of the three.

---

bosom, the self ") also recalls the word *horsain* (pronounced identically), which, for the Normands, meant "outsider."

13. Here Barney translates a verse by Shelley from memory. I have included Shelley's original verse here, as it appeared in the work *Epipsychidion* (1821). It is interesting to note that scholar David Daiches characterizes these verses as "the fullest of all Shelley's renderings of the theme of Platonic love," a topic that Barney also alludes to in her writings. David Daiches, *Critical History of English Literature*, vol. 1 (Mumbai: Allied Publishers Private Limited, 1969), 911.

Let readers draw their own conclusions based on these chemical reactions mixed with something from themselves—thus making a new set
of hypotheses—that will be equally riddled with errors!

Existence seems to be a training ground where there is more to feel
than to know—past experience never repeats itself in the same way—
and is therefore as negligible as an emotion that has lost its ability to
excite us.

PART ONE

Notes from N.'s Journal

This novel is from N.'s notebooks.[14]

The scenes and commentary in the third person come from the objective pen of her closest friend: the author.

---

14. "The heading 'Notes from N.'s Journal,' along with the division into parts 1, 2, and 3, do not appear in the manuscript itself, but rather in the original table of contents." Barney, *Amants féminins*, 41n25.

Film

Her tireless nostrils flap like wings at me (I did not know then it was by force of habit!).

"Lilith's Sin," here we are in the room of shadows, aware of our turmoil. I weakly discourage her, murmuring that we—M. and I—are too alike, that it would feel questionable, almost incestuous.

Upon leaving, fatigue overcomes me, and I lose her in the night, which she continues—by cutting her veins!

I leave on a trip the next day, without knowing anything about it. While she is dying, I live through the memory of her face and her nostrils flapping like wings at me.

Before crossing the border into Italy, I have hyacinths sent to her; I ordered blue ones, but they should have been pink.

I live through her in her country and mingle her with her native earth and sky.

I begin her through this beginning, I take root in her, aware of her maturing in me, under her sun. And I let my desire for her ripen—I do not like unripe desire.

She thanks me for the flowers, informing me that she has been very sick and is now recovering.

Easter in Florence, how can someone not be revived?

I hold her in my thoughts . . . in my life . . . she can no longer die. And I step in the shadow of the cypress trees as I pick daisies: I love her,

I love her not, I love her, I love her not . . . both are true at the same time, like the beginning of any emotion when it is still sincere.

She had asked the friend with whom I was traveling to take me to Lerici to see the rock that inspired Böcklin's painting *The Isle of the Dead*.[15] There I happened to discover Shelley's house, authentic and simple, the house Shelley left behind "to find out if the sea is indulgent and good." Why was she drawn to the dramatic chiaroscuro of a painted landscape and not to the perfect romanticism of the purest of poets? I was beginning to have doubts about her: Would she always love the obvious, the ostentatious, the flashy, the conspicuous, that external "what do I know," rather than—?[16]

I was in a terrible mood after a bumpy ride, eating lunch at three, cold *vitello*, when I glimpsed a helmeted and swollen-faced motorist—me—in the dining room mirror, evidently having survived *my best period of knighthood*.[17] And what good is it anyway to like someone who would always prefer Böcklin to Shelley?

I refrained from sending her an ironic card, since I could not find any in the whole little village that obviously derived neither profit nor fame from either Böcklin or Shelley!

---

15. Barney's text spells the artist's name as Buckler, but given the title of the painting, she is no doubt referring to the Swiss Symbolist painter Arnold Böcklin (1827–1901), who painted a number of different versions of this work, one of which now hangs in the Metropolitan Museum of Art in New York City. Barney's allusion to the work can be interpreted in numerous ways. *Women Lovers* continually comes back to the idea of death, not only in the literal sense (when M. cuts her veins or when one of Barney's doves dies) but also in the imagery that Barney uses to depict eroticism, drawing on decadent imagery from the works of French Symbolists and poets such as Charles Baudelaire.

16. It is clear in the French that Barney is referring to a famous passage in Michel de Montaigne's *Essais* in which he asks the skeptic's question, "What do I know?" (*Que sais-je?*).

17. "My best period of knighthood" is in English in the original. All words in English in the manuscript are in italics without quotation marks. There are a few instances when it was appropriate to leave foreign words in italics for emphasis as well.

I should definitely develop her artistic sensibilities—and lose weight.

I was unaware at the time that, musician's daughter that she was and Jewish down to her toes, she did not lack a sixth sense. There have been many times since then when her reaction to a work of art that strongly affected her was spot on, whether it be to a violinist she had discovered whose genius surpassed his violin, or to the view of the city of Rouen when approached from above, squeezed into the curve of its river, with its hills and its cathedrals. . . .

And at Le Select, she was the one who spotted a drunk and foul-smelling English woman poet mumbling pure miracles.

And little C., who, before falling dead drunk, stammered: "I looked for love, but failed to find it; love looked for me, but never found me. . . ."

And she was the one who wrote out on cigarette paper the (modernized) ravings of Orpheus massacred by the Maenads!

∾

Upon my return, two doomed loves are at her sickbed.

She tried to catch my eye behind the back of the friend who had returned with me.

"I have the patience of my race," she said to explain this monopolizing, "which will not last since I have come to give her a new life."

She is a white moonbeam that awakens me before daybreak. . . . I am dazzled by love, expectation, and silence.

My heart trembles before her springtime—my heart has grown new and tender shoots!

I make vows to the crescent moon. The thin moon: silver eyelash that the pure breath of my wishes has set so high!

∾

I was exasperated by the constant presence of the two Slavic women at her bedside. Not daring to complain (in any case, we are wrong to complain, for fate always has something worse in store for us!), I soothed myself by making unflattering comments about them.

N. Scrutinizes Her Rivals

D. doled out advice and paid attention like an authoritative waiter, before going to sit down with them to prove that she could outdo them. Above all, she complained about her own headache, took an aspirin, ate the supper awaiting the appetite of our patient, and then left with her scarf and Spanish hat meeting at her well-placed velvety eyes. She squinted a bit in the light, casting her gaze at the dinner guests tipsy on champagne who were awaiting "words of tenderness and affection" from her throaty voice, where every song trumpets a kind of Gypsy nostalgia. M. had been in love with D. all winter long, all the while torturing S.[18]

S. is more of a woman than D., more impure in the sense of a "sick child." S., a faux-femme with a rotten soul, had the talent to spout:

> Extracted from below, murky words
> Come from her mouth, looking like it has a red bandage on
> top
> Come from this mouth twisted by revolting births
> This mouth ultimately spills venom

---

18. The following part of the sentences is crossed out on the manuscript: "and D. is still wearing little dog collar type bracelet bearing the inscription 'I belong to S.'" In the manuscript it is unclear why this paragraph begins with "D.S." but thereafter refers to "D." We have omitted D.S. and left D. for clarity. The identity of these characters remains unknown.

And before us gives birth to its evil, drugged with opium,
    drunk with gossip.

I now understand that the Greek-Czech-Lesbian-Jewish-Russian poser
seemed like a "pure source" in comparison.

There is no "pure source"
Like the posers
With a masculine look
Who insult us?
Just as much as the feminine ones
There is no pure source
They dry up much faster.
Me, I'm a gourmet of Paris
I don't like these extremes
And even if I love to an extreme
I laugh about it!
Since I'm not fond of anything: neither the pure source
Nor proud rot

—I survive everything, except perhaps you!
Eventually the two women both left together.
But then others showed up . . . M. deflated my enthusiasm by being
fickle. Between my bed and her bed there were so many women! One
afternoon, I found her with one of my recent mistresses.

The white light no longer comes to find me in my sleep, but my angst
remains, gnawed on by doubt, grieving prematurely this pure happiness
that she will never have had and yet she already longs for.

Our passion grew amidst this confusion, but love, wounded deeply
in its subconscious, folded back on itself, could not come to fruition!
Defeated every time it appeared, love learned to keep quiet, to fold its
wings—love, the only thing that would burst joy into flames.

No trust, no surrender dared to survive the grip of possession, over and
over again. I immediately became vigilant once more, tender and distant,

as though some stranger had arrived. The flashes, the moments where we
excelled at connecting, were lost without acknowledging their existence.

She told me: "*Mon amour*, would you like my key?"

It will hurt her just as much, I realized, whether I say yes or no.

Staircase wit[19]—but there is also staircase love: mine! Each morning,
to wake her, I went up. At daybreak, in the wee hours after watching
her close her eyes, I went back downstairs: I am not one of those who
can stay!

With no trees in sight, the birds outside seemed to sing from the walls
of the houses . . .

Once when I was going home, I stepped on a red rose.

The next night, a rat went past my feet.

A happy time of superstitions and sublimations!

A happy time: a time of four-leaf clovers, of mirrors reflecting our
two heads touching, of ashtrays filled with half-finished cigarettes!

A happy time: those very first letters!

"I stay in bed day and night, waiting for YOU. *I am yours*, through
your eyes, your mouth, and your heart—and through my eyes, my
mouth, and my heart."

"My love, thank you always and forever, thank you most of all for
your tenderness and for my love. Sadly I won't be home tonight;
I am going out with two friends. Do you want me tomorrow?
To have dinner, and watch the dawn together? I will bring the
books and all of little me who loves you so much, only you."

"I leave it to you, my love whom I love, to tell me when I can see
you (a single day without you is much too long). But even if I

---

19. "Staircase wit," or *l'esprit de l'escalier*, is a set expression in French, conveying the
idea that one often thinks of a perfect comeback to something that was said, but it
occurs after the fact. Barney is also making a pun, as N. literally goes up the staircase
to see M. and leaves the same way, making this metaphor a witty double entendre.

can't see you, I do: I am all yours, in you, on you, around you, and you are in me, around me. I love you deeply, my whole being loves you—I love you."

Her letters were often accompanied by mounds of flowers that made my house into a grove.

A Tuesday Night

One Tuesday night I was feverish with jealousy when she came to me with the freshness of the *Bois de Boulogne* on her cheeks.

She begged me to become her master, to keep her to myself and all for myself. . . . And I took her again and again, had her again and again, desperate to discover the point at which she would prevent me from obeying her. I knew that by forcing her, I would lose her as surely as by granting her freedom. . . .

But she went on, insisting: "I am yours, obviously you do not understand how much I belong to you. . . . Why don't you ever ask me where I've been, where I am going? Why are you always talking to me about freedom? Be my master, since you have the power to do so . . . take me, keep me, mark me, once and for all!"

Naked, against my furs and my silks, her body was dressed in the pattern of her veins covering mine. And her body was my body, her veins my veins.

Her legs coiled around my boots that kept them apart. Her belly wanted using: drunk on slavery. And it took all the ruts of the universe to satisfy her. Her cry rose and faltered and suffered the joy of her depths: "Take me! Take me!"

. . . Then her body once again began the dance of love in my arms, renewing it again and again. I was exciting the nerves of her neck cradled in my burning palm, I drew and pushed her blood back through every blue vein. Her feet arched against my dripping thighs. And I approached to join my body's mouth to the sap that her open sex was exuding.

Oh feminine kiss, almost impossible kiss! Kiss like no other!

Insatiable—the word doesn't even capture her thirst—we also wanted the other kind of kiss. And I put her on my shoulders, seeing afar her face between the peaks of her breasts. Her face where all our sensations exploded.... And her voice rejoiced: "If women only knew! If they only knew!"

She eased herself between my lips and was at the mercy of my lips and the virility of my fingers. Emerging from the void, her belly undulated in waves between us. I was watching her—struggling, rising up, then swallowed up and lost again in her own element that was breaking over her; then her face was carried up to the summit of a deep swell and everything collapsed on the calm surface of the bed.

Love Had Entered My Home

That night one of my two old doves died in its nest. She had been sleeping separately from the other dove for quite some time, and the half-ring around her neck no longer joined the half-ring of the other dove's neck to make a wedding ring. She no longer cooed, no longer laughed with that haughty prisoner's laugh. But her smooth wings no longer knew how to fly. As a poor imitation, they spread out into the hands of my love.

Love had entered my home.

One of my two doves died that night. . . .

I knew nothing of omens!

But how could I fail to understand her! She reminded me of myself when I was young: at that age, I did not dare believe that anything could last, even pleasure, satisfied to the point of oblivion!

One day, sensing that she was going to cancel on me, I confronted her on the stairs. I wouldn't let her pass. Not even to go up those "three steps."

> My love suffers less because it is my fault,
>   That you don't come
> And also because my closed arms will help to open your arms
>   —Perhaps to another woman!

The forsaken women—turned fatalistic—and the wild young things—Bacchantes[20] of sorts—M. took up with were in the background. Or, suddenly, they became leading ladies.

And then one evening M. was so utterly disappointed that she went to the extreme of hitting her head against the walls in the entrance hall. . . .

And when I got home, I had to stop her and remove the pocketknife that she wanted to use to cut her veins again—too many steel-colored veins too close together. They were calling to the little blade as to a magnet! I struggled with her long elegant wrists to overpower her impatient veins that life couldn't always satisfy. I was struggling, my breath against her breath, my body against her body, when she changed her mind: she seized me and, from such depths of her femininity, forced a possession on me that was, unfortunately, perfect!

---

20. Bacchantes are the female followers of Bacchus, Roman god of wine and ecstasy.

How the Idea of an
"Association" Came About

Despite the fact that several woman-poets have celebrated—at the risk of distorting my reputation—the unique woman that I was for each of them—the woman in me is not my better half! M. is constantly attracted to women who are my equals (because women's capacity to be women is boundless), but she will not easily find a lover who equals me.[21]

Despite appearances, however, isn't she more attached to her lovers than I am? Or will she always prefer the woman she takes to the woman she gives herself to. . . . Even if it is the same woman?

I risked losing her in any case. But the mistress would be less inclined to cheat on me than the lover, and my feminine pride defends me against the latter. "You won't have me, you brat!" I said. "You will never have me again!"

Could I live in your perpetual "*sole mio*"?[22]

But haven't we already smiled at our excesses, when we came back together again?

---

21. The translation does not adequately convey the gender play in this line and the next. The word that I have translated as "lover" here is *amant*. It appears that N. is underscoring her masculine side, asserting that M. could find a woman who equals her, but would not find a "masculine woman lover" equal to her. For a full discussion of gender issues in the translation, see the translator's essay.

22. In Italian, this means "my sun."

At the point where a real woman rejects me, passionately communicative, and shares her ongoing need for independence—I pull myself together and diversify again. I don't need anything, except love. And the only thing that matters to me is the love that I give—(on the condition that it is well received!). This disposition allows me to be cheated on without ridicule or recrimination. May M.'s erotic destiny be as varied as those who are attracted to her!

In any case, it is as a lover that I will judge her as a lover. Being so skilled in that realm, thus able to detect even the tiniest flaw, I would counter her exaggerations to the point that they disappear. And yet love feeds on exaggerations.

And could I truly fall in love and suffer from M.'s propensity toward *don juanisme* that is so much like mine?

Youth:

Wild rose blooming in every corsage.

Anonymous excess of *appassionatas*, torrid zone where the finest metal melts, losing its shape and its image.

Fusion, confusion.

—What an avowal of love: I love you more than love itself.

Your elder, I will be the guardian of your flame, because it is the quality and the light of your flame that matter to me. And not the shivering women who come to warm themselves there, the wretched women who come to be burned!

Enclosed spaces suffocate . . . I come to save you, even from myself! Open up, here is fresh air, sun on our hands: I am your comrade!

Like a current of fresh water in the salty sea
Our secret loves, tenderly intertwined
Pass in the midst of this Godless century, with its hard way of
    thinking
And its flesh with no soul.[23]

---

23. "Lucie Delarue-Mardrus, *Nos secrètes amours* (Aurillac: ErosOnyx Éditions, 2008), 59. This is the first quatrain of 'Femmes élus.' In 1951, Natalie Barney

Alone among women, you are a unique being, and so am I . . . Let's unite—and more than just uniting—let me be with you. Let's become a double force—for Women and for us.

I will be your refuge, your safety, and your relief when one of the women torments you or hurts you.

And when one of them is tormented or hurt, let's come to her aid.

Since we love women, don't we have a duty to their sorrow and their abandonment?

We won't judge others against ourselves, and we won't compare ourselves to them either. As specialists who aren't summoned unless the situation truly calls for it, we should leave once the patient, the *love-sick*, no longer needs special care, when just anyone can continue the treatment and take over.

We are different, "more-than-women," and we are not in competition with any other woman, instead becoming her allies.

Officially authorizing infidelity removes the venom of deception. And even if I suffer because of it, even if it costs me personally, our agreement draws comfort from it—along with a recognition that protects us against any hostility!

Confined by my choice, it is up to me alone to provide the fidelity and ardor I demand.

Nothing is more lonely than love, yet don't we need company in order to stand it?

Lover of women, you whose lover I am, I propose to you the creation of an association—stronger than any union—because it includes all unions.

---

published for the first time this poetry collection that Lucie Delarue-Mardrus had written for her between 1902 and 1905. This initial publication appeared without the author's name." Barney, *Amants féminins*, 51n27. In the ErosOnyx Éditions publication of *Nos secrètes amours* (84n17), the editors note that Barney chose to place this poem first in the collection, as it paid homage to Baudelaire and set the tone for the work as a whole.

In This Country of Tenderness

The basis of our association thus established, I added this declaration in verse that M. approved.

In the country of Tenderness
We are neither Clitandre[24]
Nor some other Leander[25]

Neither Faublas the seducer[26]
Of sex, not of the heart
Nor the predatory Valmont,[27]

---

24. Clitandre is a character in love with Henriette in Molière's *Les femmes savantes*. It is also the title of Corneille's play in which appears a "cross-dressed anti-heroine, Doris." Adrienne E. Zuerner, "Disguise and the Gendering of Royal Authority in Corneille's 'Clitandre,'" *French Review* 71, no. 5 (April 1998): 757.

25. This refers to the Greek legend in which Leander swims the Hellespont in a vain attempt to reach his lover, Hero. His guiding light is extinguished and he drowns; then, she drowns herself in distress.

26. Barney here appears to be referring to the "licentious novel" entitled *The Life and Adventures of the Chevalier De Faublas*, by Jean-Baptiste Louvet (published from 1786–1791).

27. Vicomte de Valmont is a character in *Dangerous Liaisons* (1782) considered to be a libertine.

Who lives only for the chase;
Casanova,[28] Lov'lace
Whose passion tires

From the boudoir to the duel
Don Juan, more cruel
Than a homosexual.

Artificial and insipid
Are the tortures of Sade
Carnal masquerade

Of pain, stage set,
Where this innocent body
Struggles still

Beaten and decimated.
Our secret victims
—Of which I am the last—

Do sweeter evil to themselves:
Their weapons, their very own
Are of equal value.

Without murderer or crime
In deadly combat
With a rival I esteem.

With hidden meaning—vital,
Let's try the mettle
Of mental sadism.

Mark, mark as the master
The one who deserves to be mastered.
Be the one who penetrates

---

28. Giovanni Giacomo Casanova (1725–98) is remembered as the man whose
name became synonymous with libertine.

Under the bark and inscribes
Herself in the sap of the mind
With which your name nourishes itself:

The intellectual imprint
Grows, like the tree
And the initials carved in it spread.

—Love: sport which does us harm,
But without which the princes of the night
Are bored!

Women, at all costs,
Will you deign to descend
Into this country of Tenderness?

Putting It to the Test

. . . Generosity in love is expensive.

Wasting no time, M. took advantage of our association and of her new freedom . . . by throwing herself—right in front of me—at a tennis player I had brought to our bedside luncheon. . . . and she didn't have the slightest misfortune that needed consoling!

Our association existed in name only, with no real force.

My suspicions were already aroused by such imaginings—but this first encounter with reality—in a tennis shirt—hurt me so much that my throat tightened, and my heart beat harder than theirs did! To keep myself from yelling out my rage and my pain, both of which were inevitable by virtue of my entanglement with them as a couple, I got up and tried to hide my distress by pretending to write something—anything: a poem about them—for them—why not?

They were young and beautiful, and why shouldn't I limit my art to being nothing more than their "poet laureate"?

Put to the test, my theories did not allow me any kind of reproach— or the right to any obvious displeasure.

They kept on being even younger and even more beautiful—still chaperoned by me.

Every time I tried to move away, they pulled me back and seemed intimidated without me . . . Admitting to myself that I felt more inspired with some distance, I resolutely sat with my back to them and wrote:

Youth, crushing
One against the other
Laying on of hands, in prayer
Hands: the new gospel!
I believe in your veins
Fire taken from the same source
Can I warm myself in the summer day that you offer?
Or leave according to my brain and my ashes
A salamander, whole amidst your burns
I rise up like a glacier
Clad in the mantle of the moon.

After lighting a cigarette, M., a shrewd mountaineer, pointed out that glaciers descend, they don't rise.

Another time when our tennis player wandered off course into what I believed to be my personal property, I burnt her arm with the cigarette that she had given me to hold. I did it three times before she pulled it away, and cried for mercy with her hand that was hardly guilty.

Like Poor
Old House Cats

I am like those house cats that, during mating season, grow thin from having to live like alley cats.

A letter from my Dearest Friend informed me that I was neglecting her.[29] (Indeed, even if I neglect her for something that is not as important as her, don't enduring feelings sometimes serve as the steady axis around which other people wear themselves out?—Friendship is Love without pleasure.—But I didn't say without its pleasures. But as long as we have our bodies, and as long as our bodies find affinities with others, shouldn't we draw pleasure from that?)

It doesn't surprise me at all to learn that you are in love again. It saddens me that our brief trip together this spring was bound to lead to new entanglements pulling you elsewhere, and that the days we so wonderfully shared together seem to have come to an end. You are forgetting too easily that our disagreement in Italy was caused by you and not by any desire on my part to put an end to our companionship and long friendship. One of your

---

29. This refers to Romaine Brooks, who is the Dearest Friend throughout the novel. Barney and Brooks met in October 1916 and had a relationship that lasted more than fifty years. Rappazini recounts their meeting in October 1916 at a tea-party (*Élisabeth de Gramont*, 312).

meanly inspired poetic verses here, a mysterious word there, a bad
mood and impatience for no apparent reason, showed me all too
clearly that even while you were with me, you were already
yearning for the type of life that you were missing. As for me,
I return to my solitary days that are dreary, no matter where
I am. So I shall return to the sun in Italy. Will we still go to
Algeria, "*camping*" in the "countryside"[30] during the rainy season?
People who interest you don't interest me. Remember that it is
difficult to keep just one friend. Having two is often impractical.
Having three is impossible. That's because you can only be
concerned with the last one. It's never the same when you make
new friendships and new ties—it's useless to pretend otherwise—
it changes everything.

    R.

    In any case, I am still planning on spending September with
you!

Of course I know it matters to me! Only tenderness that has survived
the test of fire matters to me.

    I realize how much effort and sadness it took for her to write this
letter . . . I know this because of the tight feeling in my heart every time
I sacrifice this old friendship to a new passion—which is only a passing
phase, a love that has only one summer!

    She knew it, and I knew it, and her own past infidelities did not allow
her the right to complain, yet she still complains! And she is correct, and
what is entitlement anyway: machinery applied to our human complexities?

    And I suffer every time I stray from her door, whose wooden shut-
ters I close on her when the night falls, leaving me with the sight of her
prodigy's face against the bars of her voluntary prison.

---

    30. *Bled* has been translated throughout the novel as "little village," "country-
side," and "in the middle of nowhere." It is an Arabic word that means "village"
or, pejoratively, "hole" or "dump." Barney appears to use it exclusively in reference
to her trip to Algeria with Romaine Brooks, which was ultimately canceled.

What was she going to do with her time? Read the thick books by
Madame Blavatsky in solitude?[31] While the city lights up? I want to go
back and close that heavy door behind the two of us, rid us of all chance.
Is there no other way to be close? In such a long-standing intimacy, it is
difficult to do anything that doesn't seem excessive, *out of place* . . .
    And then, Paris meowed . . .

---

31. "Helena Blavatsky (1831–91), called Madame Blavatsky, founded the Theo-
sophical Society and was author of *La Doctrine Secrète* in two volumes (1888)."
Barney, *Amants féminins*, 56n29. In her biography on Romaine Brooks, Cassandra
Langer notes that Brooks's mother read Blavatsky: "After Mr. R.'s death, Ella
developed a devotion to the occult, and she surrounded herself with paid medi-
ums. She also became an avid reader of H. P. Blavatsky's *Lucifer*, a magazine with
a winged devil on the cover that ran articles about astral bodies and doppelgang-
ers." Cassandra Langer, *Romaine Brooks: A Life* (Madison: University of Wisconsin
Press), 19.

PART TWO

Written in the Third Person

L. Draws Closer

We are returning to Paris. . . . I long to see you . . . I want to sell
my house here, free and empty, with a pretty porcelain bathroom
and its mirrors and appliances. I would like to get 175,000 for it,
160 without commission. Maybe you know someone? Help! I
would also like to sell a beautiful brazier made of antique copper
that I have in my attic for 750 francs—maybe you will take it.
You can have it for 600 francs, what it cost us in the past, before
the carnage. I feel very happy and relieved to have fewer things.
Any kind of renunciation is an outlet for us to breathe better. . . .
We would like to take you to lunch at a little spot on the banks of
the Seine. Simply must see you soon. The pavilion is Directory
style . . . it has hot water on all floors within five minutes, a good
stove, electricity, a phone, etc. . . .

It was just like L.—incorrigibly indiscreet—to write on the envelope:
"I know that you are in love, and I know who she is . . . , but the best of
your life is *me, me, me!*"
And in another letter from L.:

I dreamt of you. We were in a convertible car, having an animated
discussion—I won't say "arguing," when a nondescript, indistinct
woman came over and tossed three bouquets of enormous rose

49

buds one after the other: white and pale-yellow roses. You asked me to go collect them; I did and awoke to the smell of roses and of your friendly face smiling at me.

What do these rose buds portend? It was pretty. I long to see you, my little darling.

I saw *Félix* by Bernstein, *Mozart* by Sacha, the Pitoieffs in *Sainte Jeanne*. I will go later on today to see Bataille's *Animateur*.

I want all my hearts—my husband's, yours, and the glances from a certain little someone—I won't show her to you—in case you take her from me! We don't show her to anyone . . .

And then, a brief, dignified letter arrived from the countryside, announcing the departure of L.'s husband with the certain little someone that they didn't want to "show to anyone"!

And the next day, on a postcard:

Completely overwhelmed by frayed nerves. I don't know what to do. Write me. Heal me from afar, and when you stop somewhere, call me. I don't regret anything. The past is dead. I have only good memories . . . but he was a man and naturally acted like a complete fool. I would like to keep my mind busy and take what little strength I have left and do something that pays (?) in the afternoons. I am on my way . . .

N. showed this note to M. who turned away: "I could never love someone who could write something like that on a postcard!"

The next day, a letter from M. to N.:

Two days is too long to go without seeing you! I'm quite depressed, and I have a thousand things to tell you. I hate all of humanity (*except you*) and especially myself. I have lost all my illusions. I got a stupid letter: my accountants aren't making any progress. With things the way they are, I really wonder if, with everything the way it is (except you of course), it is worth going on. . . . And I dreamt of L. I think that she is deeply unhappy.

Darling, forgive me, I am hurting! It hurts so much.

I am staying in my refuge all day and all night; my refuge—it is your heart and my bed.

Your M.

L. has such discipline when it comes to misfortune. Wouldn't you say that it is M. who looks like she has it worse (even though she only has minor money problems that are easily ironed out)?

N. had talked a lot about L. to M.—and she certainly knows how to talk about her.

When they saw each other for the first time, after L.'s husband had left her, M. asked outright:

M.: "And so?"

N.: "Her beautiful mouth has no wrinkles from bitterness. The contour between her nose and her lips is unsurpassed. She is of an incorrigible beauty!"

M.: "Is that all you have to say about it?"

N.: "That is the nicest thing to say about it."

M.: "And her misfortune? The misfortune that knocked her flat?"

N.: "He was discreet about it, and must have chosen some invisible place to hide. He is nowhere to be found. She seems to have banished him in their wake . . . and has only kept the words out of propriety."

M.: "He could have acted differently."

N.: "One single act is not always representative. But L. is uncompromising and makes no concessions in important matters."

M.: "Payback for having had to make so many of them in small things!"

N.: "That's her nature, feeding on extremes. . . . She includes or excludes with equal fearlessness."

M.: "I admire her for it."

N.: "A happy medium isn't glamorous, precisely because it is merely happy."

M.: "He should have stayed and stuck it out until the end."

N.: "She labels people who feign sympathy saying 'He'll be back!' as having the gossipy mindset of a *concierge*. If she receives a compliment for being courageous, she says, 'If I had given in, if I had agreed to keep them on,[32] we would have hated each other. And then there were the servants . . . we wouldn't have been able to keep anyone. I am not a libertine anymore. After this one, he would have probably wanted someone else—he was becoming lecherous and was starting to ogle girls. They would have ended up stealing my pearls and getting rid of me. It is better this way, cleaner.'"

M.: "Now she will want to have you all to herself."

N.: "L. was exaggerating when she said that the best of my life was *her, her, her!*"

M.: "You seem pensive . . . Are you worried about not having news from your Dearest Friend?"

N.: "As a matter of fact, I am—she is emotionally involved again, which is so rare for her. She wants me to stay away so that she can make the most of it a bit longer . . . and postpone our rendezvous for another two weeks."

M.: "She's not very hard to please! Tell her that you are canceling the trip altogether."

N.: "I can't."

M.: "You are going to sacrifice me to friendship!"

N.: "I don't want to sacrifice anything to anything!"

M.: "You are wrong. Remember two years ago when you telegraphed this same friend; she was disappointed with me at the time, and commanded you to join her: 'Friendship isn't love!' She was so upset after receiving your dispatch that she thought of dropping you altogether and

---

32. Here the French edition has *le*, but in the manuscript it is actually *les*. The plural is accurate here because de Pougy's husband, Prince Georges Ghika, offered for the three of them (the husband, Manon Thiébaut, and de Pougy) to live together. In her memoirs, de Pougy refers to Thiébaut as "Tiny One." Thiébaut was de Pougy's lover before falling in love with Prince Ghika. After the Prince confesses to de Pougy that he cannot "do without Tiny One," he tells her, "If you agree, nothing need change. The three of us can live together." De Pougy's sixteen-year marriage with Ghika ended when he ran off with Thiébaut. Liane de Pougy, *My Blue Notebooks*, trans. Diana Athill (New York: Putnam, 2002), 197. I have translated Thiébaut's nickname as "Tiny One" to match de Pougy's memoirs.

running away to Egypt with me. . . . All this for someone who doesn't even write you!"[33]

N.: "She did write me. I almost lost her that time, as you yourself just proved to me!"

M.: "And to think that at one point, with your hands in hers, you could have done anything you wanted me with me!"

N.: "I never noticed."

M.: "You will lose everyone!"

N.: "I act, and I can only act according to my nature. 'I cannot refuse my hand to anyone who asks for it. My life for those who love me.'"

"My life for those I love," M. corrected.

According to the terms of the "association," they were obliged to entertain and comfort L., and console her if necessary, so N. drove M. to L.'s house.

L. was there, horribly free, free like a pebble you can throw in any direction. N.'s age-old, long-standing and obsolete tenderness was called for again, to rescue L. and put her back on her feet.

L. held her mouth up to M. even before offering her hand.

"So this is the one you love," she said to N., backing off a little. "May I? Are you giving me her mouth to comfort me? You have always been my savior!" (Turning toward M.) "You have no idea what N. has meant to me, always, always. You remember the ring that I had engraved with the words: 'It pleases me so much that you suffer trying to understand and love me.' Every time I have a catastrophe or a worry that is too much for me to bear, you come and take it away . . . Oh! If I could only start sleeping again, everything would be better and I would feel alive again. Men are more of the victims of themselves than of us, my sisters . . . oh! I am with my sisters again—my sisters with such soft lips!"

---

33. Mimi Franchetti had a brief love affair with Romaine Brooks in the spring of 1925 (Langer, *Romaine Brooks*, 111).

At Le Select

Bars, just like *music-halls*, have their own local clientele, their regular celebrities, and their foreign stars.[34] A shrewd glance around the tables outside justifies saying: "It's a good house."

The members of the free circle are all present:

Downing his twentieth crème de menthe, McAc. explains how he is superior to Shakespeare to anyone who would listen.

Lady T.,[35] sitting on her barstool, loses her haughtiness by drinking *stingers*.[36]

Her pedigree greyhound ears slowly flush through her short, straight hair, and the quick pulse of her blood gradually excites the neck of her neighbors at the bar.

Her Anglo-Saxon companion blinks her failed albino eyes, with eyelashes sundrenched from being under the midnight bulbs. She stops at a

---

34. The Montparnasse café named Le Select was especially popular among artists during the interwar period.

35. This appears to refer to Una Troubridge, who frequented Le Select with Radclyffe Hall. The author Nigel Cawthorne mentions Barney and Franchetti in relation to Le Select. Nigel Cawthorne, *The Sex Lives of Famous Lesbians* (London: Prion, 2005), 140. In addition, Diana Souhami writes about Barney and Franchetti touring the "lesbian clubs," including Le Select. Diana Souhami, *The Trials of Radclyffe Hall* (New York: Doubleday, 1999), 159.

36. "A cocktail whose recipe dates back to 1915." Barney, *Amants féminins*, 63n30.

table that is as empty as a deserted island, where three friends (including N.) are calling the waiter. With lips that are even paler than her eyelids, she remains standing and lights a cigarette off of a brunette's, who has the face of a child prodigy trying to smoke like everyone else. Her ribbon, bearing the Légion d'Honneur, sets her apart and foregrounds her devotion to other work . . . N., a regular for the moment, and the violinist's boyish woman both look like they are protecting her and fearing her at the same time.

Outdoing both his violin and his boyish woman, the violinist exchanges confidences with M., who is seated with him at the next table.

An old man is slowly allowing himself to become tipsy on a blue *négresse*.[37]

A group of overly pretty boys makes the most of being next to an ugly German girlfriend who works in advertising.

A young man sitting alone, who has "what it takes to be a writer," isn't writing, but instead adds a few tears to his drink. One of the pretty boys was humming in his ear:

> Because for just one love
> I would give all my tears

A horribly Greek American man, a product of whisky and Quaker oats, is surrounded by three girls in sunglasses. He is looking to pick a fight with a couple of lovebirds, who picked up the newspaper he had just thrown away, wanting to hide behind it. The messenger appears and hands another newspaper to the American, who then sits back down with his bloodless harem.

A loud Latin woman has an English war-wounded in tow, who is using his wooden leg to protect her and keep her. Pale abject hero, he had received many contributions toward the purchase of the leg, one from the Red Cross, one from a philanthropic organization, one from his

---

37. This may have been the name of a drink at the time, or a special drink at Le Select.

father, one from the family of his ex-wife, and a few times by several regulars at the bar. At the moment this beggarly gentleman has his sights set on a once-famous dancer; the dancer is giving what flair she has left to two gullible gentlemen, pigeons who "loved her tenderly" and not disinterestedly and wouldn't let the wooden leg get his foot in the door.[38]

Thinking that she hasn't been heard, a "mime" keeps repeating, "Isn't it so, Madame, that sculpture is the future of art?"

The violinist gathers his thoughts amid the noise, closing his light-colored eyes against the bright light, sticks out his smooth chin and, without even looking, nuzzles up to M., as if up to his violin!

His boyish woman offers her glass of liqueur to N., but she isn't drinking, as usual. Just at that moment, M.'s hand—swift like an archangel's sword—swoops down in the instant between the offer and the acceptance. The glass shatters and the liqueur spills between the tables.

Lady T. gets off her barstool and leaves the counter, taking her friend with her. "Come along—leave those uncontrolled islanders!" she says in English.

The boyish woman leaves with the chevalier of the Légion d'Honneur toward his townhouse.

After their departure, N. and M. come together again; their thoughts meet up like glasses clinking to L.'s health. "She is staying up all alone," they say, like a choir in unison once again. Then, to the violinist, "Let's go, M., me, and you-and-your-violin!"

---

38. The "two pigeons" here is an ironic reference to La Fontaine's "Deux Pigeons s'aimaient d'amour tender." Where La Fontaine represents an idealistic relationship in his fable, Barney uses this play on words to depict a vulgar situation.

The Lullaby Serenade

The bars follow you with their breath all across Paris.

All that alcohol-laden breathing, after their *mixed-drinks*, their *mixed-breath*, all meet up together on the Champs-Élysées . . . the drunken shadows stumble . . . they intermingle and separate, playing in the shadows of the streetlamps.

A bell pull that you can't hear attached to the navel of a concierge (that rattlesnake must ring deep inside him!) opens up a passage whose walls slide toward a small open-aired courtyard. The unmelodic gravel—hostile to the silence of the night—crunches and is awkward to walk on. An iron shutter and a wooden door. . . . Which one to knock on? The mahogany violin case is a coffin for the child of the north, Septentrion, the North Wind, who "danced three times then died."[39] Inside the case, its body has been transformed into acoustic wood, tiny, curved like a woman's: this adolescent would have turned out badly. Someone throws off the cover and takes it from the plush interior made for its charms. It stretches out, like a child reunited with the shoulder of its master, tilting

---

39. We can surmise that Barney must have seen this monument in the town of Antibes. A stone slab from ancient Rome bears the inscription: "To the spirit of the twelve-year-old child Septentrion who was brought to Antibes for the theater, where he danced and died." "Stèle de l'enfant Septentrion à Antibes," Monument Tracker, accessed November 9, 2013, http://www.monument-tracker.com/villes/antibes/stele-de-l-enfant-septentrion/.

his head and softly thrashing it with a horsehair bow to tune it up: la-la-mi-mi . . . At once the smell of old leeks and the sound of a voice filtering from the lower window: "No music in the courtyard . . ."

But L., her torso leaning out of the ground floor window, was looking for the bell pull in the darkness. Everyone kissed her before entering.

"Oh! That's who you're bringing me?! I was afraid that it was him so I didn't want to open the door! A serenade . . . you are all so nice!"

The man-with-the-violin stayed in the drawing room but hitched the four strings of his violin to the senses and became engrossed in the music.

After Ravel's haunting *Sarabande*, Chopin's *Nocturne* was unsettling. But L. didn't understand much about music. Noise, more than sound, set her aflutter with competing emotions. Music stimulated her, the way it affects everyone else who doesn't know anything about it. She talked and talked inconsequentially, using the small vocabulary of dreams. Sprawled again on the sofa bed, her pillow looked like a wide-brimmed hat around her face. She was once again the English *Miss* with the *Keepsake* face that she always half-resembles. Wreaths of flowers sent in sympathy sprung from the ground in their invisible vases, providing a makeshift late-night *garden party* for us amongst the tarpaulins.[40]

The light from the next room shone on L., making her look younger, glinting off the enamel of her teeth and the whites of her eyes.

M. *tête à tête* and N. *corps à corps* with L.

Bach's "Air on a G String" heightened the ambience, and each stroke of the bow brought the walls down.

N. saw L. as she did before, when she loved her.

L. murmured: "Chastity and insomnia make poor bedfellows."

---

40. Even though Barney delineates certain parts of the novel as narrated from the first person and others from the third person, here she breaks from that pattern using the first person plural pronoun "us." As this novel was never published in Barney's lifetime, it is unclear whether this would have been edited in the final draft or if it represents again the blurring between the first and the third person we see foregrounded in the novel.

Transported to the past, N. was satisfied with herself and understood herself. A chill came over her body in waves, like vibratos, rising in intensity. It was like finding the familiar keys of an instrument. Her touch echoed her at her most inspired.

Completely riveted in the present moment, M. and L. were sharing one inseparable mouth. N. had thousands of hands that followed one after the other in succession along L.'s body, which succumbed in acknowledgment of the past.

In a crescendo, the palm of one hand collapsed on the great heart, and a lyrical index finger concentrated on the little heart, also in crescendo.

The vibrations of the violin strings and the body's nervous system fell into a diminuendo, sighing toward the silence . . .

L.'s sleep was comprised of so many of her different drowsy poses. N. cradled her in the vast tenderness in which she slightly envelops all women. When her love for the individual broadens into an almost universal love of the human race, she appears inspired in these moments, her words those of an apostle. It is with this voice that she corrupts wives, brings girls to tears, seduces virgins, and consoles widows.

L.'s hand lingered in M.'s and N.'s hands and her voice lingered in their ears: "Thank you, my dears, for coming to save me . . ."

One hand dropped and fell on the edge of the bed, while waves of sleep merged together with the silenced music . . .

The next day upon awakening, M. and N. received a package of sugared almonds and chocolates: "To N. and to M. L. loves you. Here are two boxes, let each choose what she wants. Here are two mouths, let each choose according to her taste. Your happy victim. You see, I am not separating you."

A Matter of Conscience

And no one thought of it as debauchery, as living like a libertine! Only those who sit on the sidelines ever have time to think about debauchery.

When her husband had proposed "living as a threesome," L. exclaimed: "But I am not a libertine!"

"And what if the Tiny One had appealed to you as much as to him?" the reasoning libertine asked her.[41]

"I would have kept her for myself," L. decided.

But since this matter of conscience had not presented itself in such an enjoyable way, L. thought long and hard about taking revenge against the memory of her husband: she would sleep with another man to atone for the crime. Her husband's place defiled once and for all, she could put it all behind her.

Motivated by the idea of finding and selecting her avenger, she accepted one invitation to go to Trouville and another to Venice.

She would often evoke this sacrificial scene:

"I will make myself beautiful. I will lie there, ready . . . He won't know who I am—because I am the one who is avenging myself. It's for me, just for me, for the peace of my body, which had been faithful to him. After that, my body as a wife will no longer exist. I will be free, free to be yours, to reclaim myself after all these men and years—and I will love only you—my dears, my sisters, my darlings!"

---

41. See note 32.

Revenge and a Trip Are Called For

That very night, M. and N. received news of L.'s departure to Trouville.

They decided to leave today. I have just enough time to finish
packing. I am only taking the essentials—you both are essential,
and you both have become the sweet memory that calms. Thank
you, my dears, think of me, speak of me. I never would have
chosen this abrupt departure, but I find we made the right
decision. You too, right? You will have to decide for me what
comes next . . . Thank you for everything, even for the tears to
come! L.

M. was shocked by this abrupt decision: "She accepted the hospitality
of this tart, and she is going to wind up in that tasteless, impersonal
clique. We need to save her. God knows whom she will choose in pur-
suing this idea of revenge that she is obsessing over. We could have at
least found a respectable man for her, like my friend M.,[42] someone that
we can trust, like my brother, my father . . ."
"Why not the Pope?"
But M. didn't pick up on N.'s humor, and concluded: "Let's go save her!"

---

42. M. is here referring to a male friend in her life, also named M.

N. retorted that L. was hardly a virgin, that she knew what to expect from men, knew how to choose them, that she wouldn't be fooled, and goodness knows what else.

M. took her mission seriously and pleaded: "Let's at least keep an eye on her from afar, breathe the same air as her. . . . It will only take us three hours to get there by car!"

"To breathe the same air" was one of M. expressions. She had already used it when she ran off to Chantilly, in pursuit of our tennis player . . .

She had many a glass of white port, waiting for the rented car and for their two bags to be brought to the door.

N. and M. set off with a compatriot who wasn't in the know, who had innocently expressed the desire to "see Trouville and die!"[43]

Very agitated, M. kept putting up and taking down the top of the convertible car, then putting it back up again. Even when her contradictory orders were being carried out, she asked if it would have been faster just to go back to Paris. If they were only halfway there, they wouldn't get there until three in the morning! But what did it matter! Only "the same air" mattered. It started to get cold. They needed to put the top back up again and continue the trip. Either the car top or the chauffeur was not cooperating, so M. tried to help. Her hand got caught in the framework of the car top and she cut open her index finger. Without a sound, she shook the shredded finger in N.'s face, and this pushed N. to her breaking point. She got blood on N.'s tie and on the only cardigan she'd brought along. Drunk on port and pain, she then threw herself into N.'s arms, shouting, "My lover, my lover!" The compatriot who just wanted to see Trouville—but not these shenanigans—didn't change her pontifical expression, which remained steadfastly fixed in the direction of the final destination for the next two hours.

The next day, they learned that L. had not yet checked into the room reserved for her by her courteous hostess. Leaving M. to breathe "the same air," as if this air would bring them nostril to nostril, N. left to spend the day in the surrounding area, full of other—and sweeter—

---

43. Barney is playing off the idea of "See Naples and die!"

memories. She came back to learn that M.'s compatriot had already packed and boarded the evening train, having seen Trouville and judged it sublime, but nothing to die for. M. had seen L. but hadn't yet "breathed enough of the same air." They needed to have dinner while watching her have dinner, and then, after dinner and two double *kummel* liqueurs, they went back to the apartment where L. was staying, while her hostess was at the casino. M. was in her best pajamas and L. was in her best night-gown (the one brought for the sacrifice?). Being in a most despondent mood, N. wanted no part in the *bed-party*. M. was shouting, "I love you, I love you" in the voice that N. knew only too well. . . . and L., with great passion, said: "Take off your pajamas."

As before when M. had taken up with the tennis player, N. sat down at a writing table and waited for the inspiration that never arrived . . . only a little quatrain to the Woman She Loved the Most,[44] with whom she had just spent the day, if only through memories of her: now, she needed to tear herself away from these memories.

> Rose of France—rose
> —Thorny irony—
> If I ever renounce you
> My eyes will remain closed!

Reassured about L.'s fate, M. set off again with N. the next day.

Passing near the house where the Woman N. Loved the Most was now living with another woman, M. said: "We should have a house like this in the country, for you, me, my chambermaid, and my cat, Bambino—our family would be complete."

A card from L. reminded us[45] of other obligations:

---

44. This refers to Elisabeth de Gramont.

45. There are moments in the third-person sections of the text where the first-person narrator reveals herself. As noted previously, it is unclear whether this was a stylistic decision to showcase the impossibility of separating the two completely or an oversight.

How was your trip back? I myself will be back soon. I am so
happy thinking about you. I have stopped crying. And the *kummel*?
(M. had sworn that she would give up *kummel* if L. would give
up tears). Your lovely faces appear before me—don't leave me
again! L.

∼

M. had taken L.'s rescue so much to heart that N., her "associate"—in
order to establish an equilibrium—resolved to let her take the lead. N.
even gave herself even over to pondering the philosophical and psychological aspects of this affair . . . What's more, she had known L. for more
than twenty years; M. for less than twenty days. It was up to M. to take
care of the sweet nothings, and N. would take care of the rest.

Since M. had already heard the story of L.'s "murder," of her "abandonment," a story L. told each time she saw old or new friends, M.
needed some persuading to go see L. when she had visiting hours. N.
even had to push her out the door after M. had arranged a time to meet
L. at a manor house on the outskirts of Paris, where the *chatelaine*—the
lady of the manor—had invited L. for the summer solstice.

M. was exhausted—she was drained of even her nervous energy after
the expedition to Trouville (from whence she brought back a fingernail
that was turning ugly, along with red eyes from the cold, both a result
of the car that wasn't acceptable whether open-topped or closed!). The
lady of the manor wasn't anyone they needed to worry about, and so
"the associates," having stifled several yawns, could retreat to their simple rooms at N.'s place in Barbizon. They left L. to collect her thoughts
in this respectable, luxurious place and take advantage of the minimum
twelve hours granted her for sleep. When N. and M. returned to take her
back to Paris with them the next afternoon, L. declared that she hadn't
gotten "a wink of sleep" and that they were wrong to make themselves
scarce and refuse the hospitality they had been offered along with her.

Digression on L.'s Marriage and on Marriage in General

In reality, L. had been feeling her husband's rejection more sharply in the countryside. They had never left one another's side until the day they left each other for good, unaware of each other, as though they had never met. Shouldn't we avoid this kind of intimacy, which always boils down to this? L. had played the role of the perfect wife . . . but was she really the wife she played? There are women who choose the wrong fate and cling to this error their whole lives.

What does she really want? Just then, nothing really. Does she want to let herself be pampered by both M. and N. and enjoy being on vacation? Or does she need a constant intimacy—one that is more and more stifling—as part of her disposition, which seeks to monopolize and destroy? Very few people are able to live on their own terms—they need someone to support their instability, and their laziness of being. But even if we grow, thanks to others, it is not because we tighten the bonds until we go numb, but rather because we allow each individual's richness to develop and grow on its own.

People said about L. and her husband: "They never leave each other's side." What an admission of weakness: Are they really so afraid to see each other, or not see each other at all, even at a distance? Or find themselves strangers with each other? Such couples don't budge for fear of interrupting the work of grafting. Each one agrees to lose his or her wholeness in order to form an unchanging, weighty block, which is as respectable as the family tomb that follows thereafter, and just as funereal. Leveling their differences doesn't even polish the surface: nothing is as cantankerous as a couple who has been together so long that they can't live without each other. Let's respect them for what they bring to life, for what we bring to life in them. But a couple is not a good judge of when it goes bad. When the couple no longer radiates its strength outward, but instead redirects it toward itself—when everything converges to serve selfishness—that's the point at which the couple enters a deadly phase that a set of habits seems to sanctify. At that moment, it's no use anymore, not even to itself. Destroyed by its own beauty, who will come to pull it out if it isn't the *third one?*

The Henhouse

The posthumous adultery that L. decided to commit in the wake of her husband's departure was put off indefinitely (to the Greek calends, or more accurately in this case, the Latin ones) until her trip to the Lido in Venice. Seeing that M. didn't like this idea and seeing that it made N. smile one of her many smiles, she spoke less about moral—and localized—vengeance. She gave herself over to her friends with demanding abandon: "I don't want to leave either of you again," she said. "I will follow you wherever you want!" "Don't leave me alone at the hair dresser." "If you don't want me to go to Venice, I won't go." "Where did you decide to go at the end of summer? Take me with you."

And it was true that M. and N. took her everywhere, even on the shortest trip or errand. One evening, N. got angry when L.'s hunger for M.'s lips could have given her L.'s sore throat. Not long after, L., irritable after a night of champagne, finally stretched out on the sofa bed and declared that she couldn't go to sleep, and that there was "nothing better in the world than M.'s lips on her lips and N.'s hands on her body." M. and N. took off their tuxedos at the same time, and laid down on either side of L., who was annoyed with N. because she had not entirely surrendered. She wanted to push N. to kneel sacrilegiously when suddenly M., as if activated by a spring, jumped up from the bed, took her things, and ran out. N., called to order, did the same thing; she likewise sprang up and followed M. as she ran across the small courtyard . . . but it was impossible to see anything other than an incoherent rage triggered by an excess of violence, and it was equally impossible to know whom M. was blaming.

When she came back, M. finally asserted: "I will no longer give myself to any woman," which explained a lot but didn't solve anything!

The next day, L. confessed that she had forced N. to act like that, and M. became, if not quite like before, at least a little more conciliatory.

L. admitted this from the bathtub; besides, she seemed distracted, as if some other more recent act needed confessing. On closer inspection, you could see that everything about the borrowed, furnished apartment looked deserted and complicit; even the infamous and intoxicated D. looked like that, drinking port after port in the antechamber. And then D. rushed into the bathroom, plunged one of her arms—stained with iodine—to the bottom of the bathtub: "I'll wash him off you!" while saying to M. and N.: "I couldn't believe my ears or my eyes . . . even when I met him, as he was leaving, he was as disheveled as the bed. When I came into the room . . ." But L.—an ancient goddess—showed them her shirt on which her disgrace was evident, and said: "Wanting to vomit as much as I wanted to cry, I drank!"

L. let herself relax into the warm water of her bath, her vengeance complete. It no longer mattered to her. This act now seemed so ordinary, merely a last-minute decision with a suitor from her past who had come to give her his condolences—and he had willingly obliged her.

After D. had sponged her down following this *round*, she dried her off, put perfume on her, and said: "L., don't forget that I am coming for you tomorrow to spend twenty-four hours in my country house." Upon saying this, she glanced askance toward M. and N. with an evil eye, and left.

Pensive and gloomy, M. said nothing because she had so many things to say. N. became serene once more and smiled a new smile, but didn't say anything either. But this was because she wasn't thinking about anything. L. said less than nothing, because her body language said more, and because she felt good and sleepy.

All evening, M. took care of L. like a new bride . . . and took her home at ten o'clock. She joined N. at Le Select at midnight, with the good news that L. "was sleeping."

Two Kidnappings

N. was still asleep around nine in the morning when a key arrived from M., with a note giving a vague explanation. For the first time, N. sensed betrayal and lies:

> Some friends are taking me to the countryside for lunch, and
> I don't know where we will go after that . . . I can come to your
> place tonight around 10:30 p.m. or you can come to mine after
> dinner. Here is my key!! Tenderly and deeply yours, M.

N. replied: "I will come to your place. *Tenderly*, but there are days without tenderness. *Deeply*, but there are evenings without depth. N."

Like those who have a radio at home, N. was able to follow M. on the road chasing L. at D.'s house. . . . Because N. was on the outs with D., M. didn't dare tell N. about her plan to prevent L. from spending the night in that horrible house. At that very moment, D. was probably flirting with M., saying bad things about N., and trying to keep them from leaving . . .

After midnight . . .

M. came home with an angry pout, looking trapped.

M. said: "L. slapped me because I said something bad about you . . . I am sick of hearing her put you on a pedestal . . . you and your famous hands!"

N.: "Did you bring her back from D.'s?"

M.: "Of course I did—she couldn't stay the night in that brothel."

N.: "?"

M.: "She doesn't want to see me without you, or there are always lots of people around. When no one else is there, she calls her attending lady[46] so that she doesn't have to be alone with me!"

N.: "I thought that you loved her for her loyalty most of all?"

M.: "Everything has its limits."

N.: "?"

M.: "And to think that there was a time when you could have done anything you wanted with me!"

N.: "I never noticed."

M.: "I want a woman for myself, just mine—do you understand?"

N.: "That's what I do understand . . . it could be L. or someone else . . . but she is better than someone else. She is a good influence on you. I will tell her . . . to help you . . . I promise that she . . ."

M.: "I don't want her anymore—she doesn't appreciate the honor I am paying her . . . I have everything to offer . . . she has only her old age."

N.: "I thought you especially liked older women?"

M.: "She is not the only woman in that category! . . . The princess of A. I will go see her . . . My brother won out over me last time, but she must have thought about it since, and regretted it . . . she should be ready for women by now."

N.: "Enough of foreign stocks, balance your budget! You have too many Slavic and Hungarian shares: try a few good French bonds!"

M.: "They only yield 3 percent!"

N.: "So, you choose a risky speculation where you have everything to lose! Why not D.?"

M.: "Yes, why not? As a matter of fact, she is coming to have tea along with Bêlenosse tomorrow."

---

46. Liane de Pougy became royalty upon her marriage to Prince Ghika in 1910; as Princess Ghika, she traveled with an attending lady.

N.: "Goodnight! You will need your rest before trying to corner that market! Do you want a tip on how to go about it? I know D. by heart, through others' hearts."

M.: "Everything that is happening is your fault!"

N.: "And everything that isn't?"

M.: "Is your fault too."

N.: "*Amen!*"

M.: "You know, you only have one kind of purity, one freshness: your mouth, but only when you don't talk. But when I think of how you gave it to her . . ."

N.: "But my mouth is yours! Do you want it for the same thing that I do?"

M.: "Your mouth—without words?"

Then N. took the last pink candle and shut the door softly.

Secret Service

Nine in the morning: N. is on the telephone.

N.: "Laborde 03-11 . . . L., is that you?"

L.: "Yes . . . oh, hello darling! You know: M. was unbearable last night . . ."

N.: "Yes, I know . . . But you still shouldn't have sent her D's address. We need to keep her to ourselves—even if she is unbearable. D. and her circle are just appalling. M. is too easily swayed both by good and bad influences. I don't want to see my 'associate' get caught up in all that."

L.: "What should we do?"

N.: "Be less . . . loyal to me! Have lunch with M. today and prevent her from going home afterward . . . D. is meeting her there for tea."

L.: "Really? I had refused to have lunch, but. . . . all right . . . you can count on me. I will keep her from going! And we will come see you . . . afterward . . ."

N.: "L. . . . you know . . . it is difficult to say . . . especially on the phone. Don't forget our pact. That's the one thing that I cannot put up with."

L.: "I remember the ecstatic look on your face when you held M. close . . . without being seen. It was only a flash . . . but I know you and I understood right away! Besides, doesn't every paradise need a forbidden fruit?"

An Announcement

From L. to N.

Here is a stick to beat me with and a snake skin found under the
roses of paradise.
    Words, gestures, decisions, impulses, regrets—in a word, all of
life! Your L. (who is leaving all the same for Venice)

~

From M. to N.

I Iello—I will certainly come today at one, but only because I
have a hankering for American-style chicken. There . . . But I am
pouting. M.

L. Leaves to No End

They look good together . . . seeing them makes even people hurrying to catch the train turn around and do a double take. They are a good-looking—and modern—couple. L. is holding M. by the arm, her hand heavy with pearls: M. had added a wedding ring. They are both wearing similar fitted jackets. They are walking in stride with each other. M. looks like a *jettatura*,[47] with her pale complexion of the Israelites, and her head, like Saint John's, appears decapitated by the reddish scarf she wears on special occasions.

Less expressive, L. is only white from powder and pearls. Her face—that of a Christian led astray who remembers having been a courtesan—rises above her necklaces. More beautiful than her pearls, her iridescent face rules them.

N. follows behind them, her blond hair a mess; she is shorter, and her soft smile is dominated by her willful nose and hard, darting eyes that "carry with them the discomfort of their own sincerity."

No physical trait seems to link the three women; there is no visible sense of togetherness to reveal how close they really are.

So the ticket collector hesitated: "Madame, if you are with these ladies, please come forward. If not, step back and let them through!"

---

47. This word with Italian origins can be defined as "a curse of the evil eye, whereby all that the cursed looks upon will suffer bad luck." *Collins Online Dictionary*, s.v. "jettatura."

L. laughed, and to further emphasize their connection, leaned out of
the train to N. and kissed her, whispering in her ear: "Take care of M.
for me just as I would for you . . ."

Like two comrades in love, N. and M. started home, at ease alone,
without formality.

Then, the next day, they spent thirty-six hours in two rooms across
from a bar in Barbizon, where the American bartender mixed them *mint-
juleps* at four o'clock and, in the evening, made the dark *stuffing* with chest-
nuts—M.'s favorite—to go with the chicken.

As usual, M. had filled the rooms with flowers, provided by the elderly
owner who had taken them from her vegetable garden. There were two
exceptionally beautiful, enormous red geraniums in their pots, real little
roses with fragile stems, and a few jasmine flowers floating like stars in
the water jug, surrounded by rosemary and verbena leaves.

Everywhere she went, M. always wanted to spruce up and beautify
the bedrooms, so she nailed a green-and-white checkerboard above the
best bed. She was glowing with good will and kindness. Hammer in
hand, she worked diligently, improving the wall that repaid her with the
image of her shadow kneeling at the place consecrated to pleasure and
sleep.

M. woke up next to N. like a colt neighing, happy to be turned out to
the green pasture! They felt momentarily drawn to walks in the forest,
boat trips, and all kinds of sports: horsing, tennis, swimming—but all
they did was walk down the main street. N. went to buy barley sugar
from the nuns in Moret, and M. bought all kinds crazy knickknacks
from the antique dealer.

They called the bistro to see if M.'s concierge had any dispatches.
When they found out there were two, M. went home . . . read them and
left again for Barbizon. This distant call prevented M. from calming
down. She felt that "something bad was going to happen," and her imaginings kept her awake: what if her mother was dead, killed by a crazy
person . . . what if L. was demeaning herself at disgraceful parties—and
was having such a good time that she would never come back—or would
return when it was too late!

They needed to go home. A supremely ordinary letter was waiting for M. It was a bit harsh toward N. (L. must not have thought that N. would read it).

M. got angry that this letter satisfied neither her curiosity nor her anxiety. She thus responded with a letter that was even more supremely ordinary, which could at least serve to restore her pride and maybe even bring back the "abandoned woman's" love. L. would be sure to share it with her entourage, as she always did. Just like at the theater, where our[48] famous women's adventurous love lives belong to the public.

Their pact set M. and N. on a campaign to find yet another Newly Miserable Woman.[49] Fortunately, she was still in the company of the woman who had become unworthy of her and from whom she needed saving. Faithful to her pact with L., N. was relieved about this white lie that pushed M. back toward Venice.

L. was a beautiful item on sale that had fallen off the matrimonial counter at the end of the season—and she would be carried off the highest bidder.

M.: "We never should have let her leave. You have no idea how much I love her."

N.: "You don't either!"

M.: "Why don't I love you the way that I love her?"

N.: "Probably because that would suit her even less—and wouldn't suit me either!"

M.: "You are crazy with pride, you never let up . . . but I will conquer you, just like the others. That will be the greatest feather in my cap."

N.: "Everything becomes you . . . , but I will give you more than feathers."

---

48. As seen previously, the first-person plural possessive "our" is an intrusion in this third-person section of the narrative.

49. Jean Chalon was able to confirm that this is none other than Djuna Barnes. Jean Chalon, pers. comm., September 2013. It would seem that this reference to the Newly Miserable Woman (*La Nouvelle Malheureuse*) is the same as the interlocutor at the end of the novel in the dialogues. Because initials are so significant in this novel (see Hawthorne's introduction for further discussion), her name is translated to preserve the initials in the French, which are N.M.

M.: "And if I can't make you suffer enough on my own, I will do it through someone else: the Woman You Loved the Most. I will woo her and win her over, and erase her memory of you."

N.: "Do it, if you can."

M.: "But in the meantime, L. is going to attend that *bal masqué.* I want to leave tonight, to see her again, to prevent her from . . ."

N.: "From having fun?"

M.: "Yes—there is something better—me!"

N.: "Get her involved in an affair that will last another eighteen years?"

M.: "Yes, that's right. I will replace the man who deserted her. I will devote my life to her. The woman who was your first love will be my last."

N.: "Your idea is a bit monotonous for me!"

M.: "You are never serious—but I always am."

N.: "But doesn't that turn out to be the same thing? My 'associate,' our amorous friendship is more real, and purer, too . . ."

M.: "I know that. It was so wonderful to be yours—to be with you—with them! Why did you put that woman in my head? My imagination is on fire . . . I need to leave . . . come with me! Keep me from leaving!"

Delayed!

N. obeyed and hid M.'s passport when she left. Her only reward was receiving this complaint upon awakening:

> *Darling*, please . . . give me back my passport—I cannot bear it any longer and must leave. Otherwise, I will leave for good. You know, N., this pain is from you, and now it's in me . . . and well? still? It still comes from you—from your imagination, from your masochistic pleasure—so then—what?
>
> P.S. Would you be so good as to lend me 10,000 francs for my getaway? Oh my!

N. had to rely on her exceptional flexibility and wisdom to bring this getaway into perspective.

"I am not the one who is bothered by this trip (even though I hate traveling). I will go see how my Dearest Friend is doing—you are the one who said that this would make things very difficult for you."

N. sent a telegram to L. telling her to come back, right in front of M. She stopped the trip before it even started, just as the chauffeur was reserving two sleepers for that night.

L. was either panicking or getting bored in Venice; she replied by saying that she would return in three days. M. regained her patience and good mood, and even—perhaps—found a mistress for a fling! No, but in any case, L. promised the "Newly Miserable Woman" N.'s comforting charms because they were "both women of letters and Americans" and because things with M. could only end in a banal "zoom zoom" that wouldn't fix anything in this life that needed doing over. Once the collapse of the Newly Miserable Woman's current relationship was definitive, they would have to see . . . because M. really liked her. She had already paved the way one rainy night in the *Bois* . . . maybe she would take advantage of it the following winter!

Intersecting

Now it was L.'s turn to overuse the telegraph poles whose wires always seemed to be quivering under this onslaught of good or bad news. Puvis de Chavannes[50] depicted it by two classical dancers on a rope, one dressed in white and the other in black. The latter's face is covered, no doubt to distinguish between the bad and good news that travel these lines of communication.

"L. is seriously ill at Hotel Leman, Ouchy."—N., love, I am going absolutely crazy, I just received six letters from L. and just got this telegram.—I am leaving for Lausanne. I am waiting for the train to leave. Love, will you come? I feel like I am dying of fear. Can you see my dread? I knew it—I did—please come right away, you are the only one who can give me a moment of calm and patience . . . Please come, come help me decide, I will hold two seats in case.—It would take too long in the car!

On the train, N. found M. to be in a diabolical mood. It upset M. to be so worried, and it upset her to leave her bed . . . to leave, perhaps to calamity.
M.: "If L. dies, I will kill myself. I'm an idiot . . ."
N.: "That's not what this is about . . ."

---

50. Pierre Puvis de Chavannes (1824–98) was a French painter.

M.: "She is so ill that she can't even send a telegram herself . . ."

N.: "That's true—it appears to be the case."

M.: "Things were so good with you . . . idiot, idiot—why don't I love you instead of L.?"

N.: "I am here . . . I will always be here . . . aren't we alike?"

M.: "Idiot. . . . I'll be stuck for months, maybe even years. I'm going back to the shadows. I know what it is like. But the distance between you and me is great. I will catch up to you."

N.: "Shall I wait for you at the end of the tunnel?"

M. took this metaphor the wrong way: "So you won't come with me? Then I will only have my chambermaid, this outsider whom I don't trust to bring back our two coffins—if something bad happens—bad things come in twos! Idiot, idiot . . ."

N.: "They come in threes!"

M.: "Idiot, idiot, idiot . . ."

Just as she had done before the expedition to Trouville, M. drank port after port. The tone of her cursing heightened to the point of the burlesque, and even a hint of subtlety had no chance of slipping in. M. had drunk to the point that she thought a very showy woman in the dining car "looked really good" . . . To punish N. for having hesitated to come with her right away—without having called Lausanne—she retired for the evening to her compartment with her chambermaid, where N. watched her in the shadows during a dark, sleepless night.

Once they got off the train, they felt reassured by the reasonable and tidy little atmosphere of Switzerland, where it seemed that nothing truly terrible could happen. Sure enough, L. was confined to bed with a mild case of bronchitis. In need of patients, the doctor had declared it to be "perhaps quite serious." This same doctor was now smiling, as everything was already "perfectly under control."

N. grumbled a bit because she had left in haste the day before the Woman She Loved the Most was meant to be coming through Paris.

"You're angry with me for not being on my deathbed, then! I think she would have preferred to find me dead!" said L. turning over toward M.'s side to elicit more sympathy.

As if recovering from a big shock, M. remained completely unemotional. L. coughed, spit, and tossed and turned in her bed, a little bit vexed: "You suggested the trip to Lausanne for your sore throats—I thought that this would be a nice change for you." And then, speaking to her attending lady, she said, "Wasn't I terribly sick in the train as we were leaving, and just as sick when we arrived?"

The baths seemed so wonderful and the lunch was so unremarkable that the travelers were back on their feet in no time. They were in such a good mood that they started planning a boating trip. M. and N. would row with the convalescent L. lying at the helm.

"And then we will leave on the train the day after tomorrow . . ."

"No, let's take the car, I love driving!"

"If the doctor could see you now!"

"There is nothing that heals faster than great happiness," L. explained. She was still a bit contrite, because the Woman N. Loved the Most had heard her healthy-sounding voice over the telephone and had sent a postcard reminding her of the Boy Who Cried Wolf.[51]

A sacrifice being needed to appease the gods, N. had M.'s extra chambermaid locked up in the Lausanne prison; she had stolen one hundred Swiss francs from M. With the help of a cashier who was her lover, she'd probably also stolen two travelers' checks of fifty francs each.

The attending lady returned home alone with the tickets and the bags. L., M., and N. were alone.

"The rest of the world can vanish. The two people dearest to me are here with me," M. said to N. with a quiver, but N. did not share this same feeling of exclusivity.

---

51. "This must refer to Aesop's fable 'The Boy Who Cried Wolf.'" Barney, *Amants féminins*, 87n34.

Three Returns

N. had telegraphed her Dearest Friend to find out if she was ready to meet her on the other side of the Alps. She responded that she still needed to visit a number of people before leaving Italy and asked N. to meet her after mid-September, stating that she would write "more explicitly from Paris."

"Give up on the 'little village' in Algeria," said M.

N.: "I never give anything up!"

M.: "I won't like knowing that you are so far away . . . you were the one, after all, who arranged for me to spend a whole month with L. all by myself."

N.: "I often set things up that I cannot stand—so that I can learn to stand them!"

L., M., and N. set off in the car on the road around Lake Geneva that was as quaint as a bridle path. That night they arrived at some unbelievable mountains. The next day, L. had vertigo when they went back down the windy mountain through vegetation that looked like something out of a cubist painting—it was swaying. Kissing was still forbidden, and so L., acting immature, and M., teasing in a childish way, were taking great pleasure in keeping silent until one of them spotted seven cows. This was an easy game, because the mountain was teeming with these dappled animals. The whole mountain was singing a traditional Swiss cow-calling song. Like an artist in love, M. cried out when she saw a granite outcropping

that, from a certain angle, looked like L.'s profile. The first words she spoke
were: "Oh! How wonderful it would be to set your face into this rock!"

Every evening, as luck would have it with hotels—which were all
fine—M. and N. slept in the room with two little beds while L. was in
the room with the large bed. The door between the rooms was left ajar,
giving the impression of a dormitory full of well-behaved children! Each
day of travel was a half hour too long, and this made them too tired to
act upon any sensual desire. The long days, combined with the fresh air,
lulled them to sleep very early in the first bed they found.

As soon as they descended the plains and found wonderful food, their
spirits were lifted. L. and M. planned out the month they would spend
together when N. would finally join her Dearest Friend in the South,
who was returning from Italy to go with her to Algeria.

The ominous and promised "little village" in the middle of nowhere
was in sight.

"Try to make up . . . find the right combination . . . this is your
forte . . . Don't go so far, just stay long enough in the South to check
your house under construction![52] We will go with you as far as Avignon.
And then you can come get us in Brittany with your car . . ."

Certainly not in "the house of the betrayal."[53]

---

52. Barney was having a house built in Beauvallon with Romaine Brooks. It
was called the Villa Trait d'Union (the Hyphenated Villa) because it consisted of
two separate units joined by a common dining room. The idea of a hyphen is also
important in *Women Lovers*, as the "third one" symbolically plays the intermediary
role, like a hyphen. Later in the novel, Barney represents the evolution of the
relationships between the three women using a hyphen.

53. "The house of the betrayal" appears to refer back to Prince Ghika's betrayal
of de Pougy with Manon Thiébaut at the house located in Roscoff, Brittany.
Another love triangle also took root in this same house, between de Pougy, de
Gramont, and Barney. This incident shares parallels with *Women Lovers*: de Gramont
and Lily became enamored with each other and Barney was jealous, even going
so far as to ask de Pougy not to see de Gramont alone, a directive that she did
not follow! For an account of these events, see Francesco Rapazzini, *Elisabeth de
Gramont: Avant-gardiste* (Paris: Librarie Arthème Fayard, 2004), 390–92. The English
translation of this biography by Suzanne Stroh is forthcoming.

"Perhaps it is better to create new memories to erase the old ones? M., do you want to?"

Yes, she did!

M. and L. drew closer to each other, holding hands, and got very quiet, as if they were already alone!

While she was watching this, N. began to think about her role as the "third wheel."

"What is N. thinking about?" L. and M. said, both feeling neglected.

"I am thinking of thought itself, pure thought."

The Third Ones

The third ones are born out of the couple: they follow the natural law that one and two make three.[54] Some third ones are born predestined: but others are accidental, through chance or circumstance, occasional thirds—but they don't stay that way. They become part of a couple and disappear, until another third one comes and replaces them. Almost everyone belongs to this type—there are very few who are the pure type of third one.

There are several types of third ones. There are the hunchbacked 3s, the uniform Roman III, the ▽ of a triangle, the ♡ of hearts, and the divided ♀ ☿ of the clover, and the ☡.[55]

The third one can turn into the first, and the first can turn into the third: trinities are interchangeable. The best position, but the most difficult to maintain, is the one in which *there are three but no one is the third!*

The couple is either a struggle for supremacy or else the suppression of one person; the couple can at times accommodate a third one, who

---

54. In the original table of contents, the title of this chapter appears as "La philosophie du *troisième*" ("The Philosophy of the Third One").

55. "Barney drew the figures listed on the typed manuscript. The last one is ambiguous: is it the letter Y, a helix, or something else? In the previously mentioned *Le Manuscrit autographe* (98), this figure is called a triskelion." Barney, *Amants féminins*, 90n37.

becomes an insulator or a hyphen between the two (as in the cases when a hyphen dignifies certain words, such as "well-loved," etc.). In everything that is balanced, the balance of the trinity is the most perilous. Either the two become so close that the insulator becomes an intruder, or the hyphen is suppressed or crushed . . . in its simplest expression, it is reduced to a line that is no longer in suspension, a line that no longer separates them, a line thrown away, a simple dash on the ground __, leading nowhere.[56]

As we know only too well, the third one has multiple uses. An extra horse on rugged climbs. A belay during difficult descents—unnecessary on a plateau where there's momentum and everything is going smoothly. But when the couple's journey becomes hilly once more, the third one is quickly called to the rescue.

We are interested only in the exceptional third one—in exceptional cases.

The triple law of a trinity is that none of the three be the third. But everything that the two beings take away from the third for themselves diminishes the latter.

The couple is a noose—whose members tighten the bond—and so the third one is forced to be brilliant and to find a raison d'être when all is lost! Or abandon the game altogether.

So the third one, realizing that she is being left out, resolves the situation by putting her loneliness aside, as it has become useless . . . or, without suffering, she infuses the space like water. Water never suffers, escaping any amorous stranglehold.

The couple is like the two-headed monster Scylla and Charybdis,[57] the fatal sea hazard. Deep water at high tide is the only safe passage between them.

---

56. The French publication of the novel does not follow the manuscript in that there is an underscore line in the original, which the translation includes. For a discussion of the hyphen in this novel, see note 52.

57. Scylla and Charybdis are two monsters from Greek mythology who appear in Homer's *Odyssey*. They are dual perils (in popular usage, they are joint dangers; i.e., if one doesn't get you, the other will).

But how few venture there: you'd have to be like a ghost—endowed with immateriality—to do that!

The third one becomes the third at the very moment of her suppression—or her alliance. If she knows how to wait, before long she will become either the Intruder or the Leader. Love is heavy for two to carry, and happiness is monotonous.

Leaving as those who are simple and pure are wont to do, she ruins any chance for a triple happiness—and the possibility of variety. Yet variety is the very best thing for this celestial parasite to feed on, mistaking it for heaven.

It is then that a Satanic element enters this close combat—which tempts and drives the couple out of their Eden—and also infiltrates their ranks to lead them as they go astray. Having been the Presumptuous One, the third one now becomes the Unique One.

We are inhabitants of a three-dimensional space we cannot fathom. The Whole remains unknown to us. We are confronted with the creation and dissolution of a continuity.

Tenacious and possessive just like Dante's Paolo and Francesca,[58] who lose themselves in their union, becoming eternal in the Hell of Exclusivity. Or connected and in agreement like the Three Graces; as they age, they become the Three Fates, who freely pass the threads of destinies among themselves.[59] They are three equals, but can there be equal parts? Would the third woman have the best part of it?

In order to be third, you need to be the strongest of the three. You must be all three, all that the third one encompasses.

But who will speak of the third one's hell, of the strength of her fire? No concession, no respite! You always need to go beyond yourself. Or

---

58. "Lovers from the Middle Ages whose guilty passion leads them to death. Dante, *Divine Comedy*, canto 5." Barney, *Amants féminins*, 92n38.

59. Barney includes numerous references to Greek mythology, underscoring its importance in her intellectual development and her literary works. Here, the Three Fates hold the threads of each person's life. When Atropos cuts the thread of a person's life, s/he dies.

how are the others to follow? Always at risk of being left behind, the third one needs to be as charming as an angel.

What lover's tears are worth the dew from her eyes?

Exposed and re-wounded again and again in her vulnerability, she finds her raison d'être—and is forgiven for her wounds that sing.

A recondite love sunk in its joys comes to life and listens to her.[60]

60. "Barney put her signature, 'Natalie Clifford Barney,' at the end of this chapter." Barney, *Amants féminins*, 92n40.

N. Returns to
Less Pure Thoughts

Pure thought is easy . . . let's come back to our human condition, returning to our unacceptable and difficult thoughts. What have we not failed to do . . . so that we might fail!

The love between M.[61] and L. deepened, took shape, became flesh . . . Their departure neared. So did N.'s.

Hearts are not made to simply beat in time—but instead out of time—arhythmically! That is how N.'s heart beats.

The intensity of her solitude already rivaled L.'s and M.'s intensity as a couple.

Occasionally they brought N.—love's orphan—along with them to lunch or dinner. M. had changed restaurants in these eight days as often as she used to change women. L. and M. were behaving badly. It hurt N. to be with them . . .

M. had stopped drinking and went to bed as soon as she tucked L. into bed. She became exemplary, unrecognizable, almost chaste: and one day, she spoke of the amorous friendship she felt with L. Upon hearing this, L. sulked the entire day.

In the evening, when M. was heading out to buy newspapers at the kiosk, L. didn't want to leave her side, not even to sit in the car and wait

---

61. The French edition's typographical error with the names (Barney, *Amants féminins*, 93) has been corrected in the translation.

for her: "We can't leave her by herself for one minute—someone might take her away from us. Some woman, some passerby, might arouse her interest . . . who knows! It happens so fast. From here, we can watch her."

N.: "You are that taken by her?"

L.: "She has all those qualities I love. But listen, tell me—quickly—if you want me to, I can still stop. I love you the most . . . I don't want to you to suffer. Tell me if you want me to leave . . . if you want me to go and hide . . . at your house in Barbizon, for example, or somewhere else. She won't even know where I am, and you will be there to prevent her from doing something rash. She will forget me . . . it's still not very . . . Tell me if that's what you want! And if it is painful for me, I will tell myself that it is for you, so that you have less pain than I do. It would be sweet to suffer and sacrifice myself for you . . . Is that what you want?"

N. was more moved than L., so moved that she couldn't speak, so instead shook her head "no," as if to say "everything was fine like this."

So M. and L. withdrew. Full of concern, M. instinctively leaned toward L. and took her in her arms. And L. left feeling relieved, happy that she had accomplished her noble deed—at least in words . . .

L. is capable of moments of deep devotion, but how many times have there been when she almost didn't become aware of it in time . . . For now, let's not reverse the roles: an instinctual monopolizer, L. will always play the one who takes everything, and N. the one who has everything to give!

Priest Baltazar Gracián's advice is wise: "Avoid those who are unhappy."[62] But, unfortunately, N. was beyond wise!

And even if N. had been able to hide her precious M.—would she have lost her any less?

---

62. Baltazar Gracián y Morales (1601–1658) was a Spanish Jesuit known for his work entitled *The Art of Worldly Wisdom*. This collection of maxims must have appealed to Barney's literary sensibilities, as she was a master of *pensée*. Indeed, her published *pensées* are among her best literary works. See Barney's three collections of aphorisms: *Eparpillements* (Paris: Sansot, 1910; rpt. Paris: Éditions Geneviève Pastre, 1999); *Pensées d'une Amazone*; and *Nouvelles pensées de l'Amazone* (Paris: Mercure de France, 1939). Translated excerpts of these works are available in *A Perilous Advantage: The Best of Natalie Clifford Barney*, trans. Anna Livia (Norwich, VT: New Victoria, 1992).

L. told her over and over: "I'm keeping your treasure for you." But in what way?

And M.'s voice echoed, jeering: "Idiot, idiot, idiot!"

One of the last evenings that she had dined alone with N., she ate neither the onions à la crème nor the salad with chives (that she loved), and she didn't touch the wine. She had her coffee and left at ten o'clock, shrouded in mystery—she thought!

The next day, white gladioli worth a bridal song arrived, along with this note from L.:

N., darling, here are some flowers, put them near you, you that
I love so tenderly, you who has done everything in the world she
could to heal me. Oh my darling, I feel so many things—many,
many, *many*. Thank you for guiding the movement of my life after
I was stabbed in the back. I am coming back to life . . . I've almost
lost my fear of coming back to life. Thank you for the tenderness
of your sacrifice—your sacrifice that will also be mine. Darling,
I love you. All that is brutal is natural—all that is tender is
superhuman. My dear, my sweet little one, I am able to live out
this beautiful dream because of you (you know, of course, what
you are to me?) Shall I awake? And if I do and you are no longer
there, I shall not want anything other than God! Your L.

Every day, N. watched M. give a little more of herself and L. take a little bit more. L. knew how to reach her, to surround her, how to draw her out, how to touch her and how to move her. Full of pride, N. held her head high without flinching.

The strong will always be defeated by the weak, and they will carry their suffering for them—they will taste the soil of defeat and chew their ashes at night. The weak will take away the loves that they cherished and the sweetness of their honeymoons—after the tears! But nothing will console the strong, not even their own strength used against them!

Balance Sheet

N. went back over the campaign that L. ran from the beginning; she took note of several particularly suspicious times so as not to get lulled into believing so strongly that L. had ever been acting in good faith. So as to avoid succumbing to gullibility—even for a moment—she found bitter satisfaction in L.'s two-faced assertions. L. was saying:

To M.: "But I can love only if I believe that it is forever!"

To N.: "This is whom you love? You are bringing her to me to comfort me? You are lending me her mouth?"

To M.: "What an attractive couple we make! Everyone turns to look at us . . . I know very well that . . . but you would rather be with me!"

To N.: "I don't want to separate the two of you." (Actually, since returning, N. almost never sees M. alone.)

To M.: "Yes, give me your wedding ring. You are worth much more than what I lost."

To N.: "I won't let her drink or cheat on us and I will give her back when you return. I am keeping your treasure for you."

To M.: "I would like to find someone to sleep through the night with, and I believe that I could with you. I was not physically attracted to my husband—but I am to you!"

To N.: "I will leave and hide, if you want me to. She won't even know where I am."

To M.: "Is there an apartment in your building for me, so that we won't have to be separated during the day either?"

To N.: "Besides, she will get sick of me within a week and will write to you: '*Help! Help!*'"

To M.: "I also had a wedding ring made for you and I wanted to put it on your finger before our honeymoon tomorrow. No, no need to pay for your ticket . . . you are mine and I am taking you home." (The scene about the rail ticket and then the reconciliation lasted until ten o'clock at night while N. was waiting for M. to come for dinner.)

To N.: "Of course I will tell her that I need to get ready, so that you can have some time with her before we leave. Then you will come join us and I will always have your room ready, right next to M.'s. I won't see her again until the train station—I don't want to interfere with your goodbye dinner!"

M. apologized for being late: at the last minute, a telegram had informed her of an imminent inheritance—and she had gone to tell L. about the telegram.

The letter from the Dearest Friend arrived the next day asking N. if she could postpone their trip until the end of September: "Algeria will be more beautiful in October . . ."

N. had guessed right! "She was getting emotionally involved, something unusual for her, and she wanted to savor it a bit longer."

L. and M. were already together when N. went to announce the news. M. bit her lip so that she wouldn't let something careless slip. But L. said halfheartedly: "It's too bad you didn't know sooner . . . The house is in a terrible state . . . I don't dare have you come right away . . ."

N. reacted out of pride and pretended that her trip with the Newly Miserable Woman was already set and that she could no longer put it off . . .

After running errands, they all had lunch together, glum and awkward.

Then L.—who always needed two hours of rest after lunch—arrived with her bags after a little twenty-minute nap.

L. and M. Leave Together

Dismayed by the crescendo of the last twenty-four hours, N. pretended to have to meet the Newly Miserable Woman, so as not to see L. and M. leave together. She took her leave.

Perhaps L. was starting to realize that she was being as attentive to M. as she was not being to "her rescuer" now that the rescue was complete; in any case, L. had her loyal attending lady join N. in the antechamber to let her know that "L. really cared for her." That was exactly what the "Tiny One" said to L. when the "Tiny One" was leaving with her husband! Was it perhaps necessary to remind L. of her retort at the time? L. had said: "You have a funny way of showing it!"

N. felt a strange kind of relief at the thought of not having to see L. and M. again just after she left, relief at having some space between the three of them. They were making each other's heads spin—and were stepping on each other's toes.

And then, in an impulse she didn't act on, N. saw herself—feverish and drowning in tears—shoving the two of them into each other. To push them together all the more—hadn't she pretended to have a meeting with the Newly Miserable Woman that very evening, a meeting that prevented her from having one last dinner with them and seeing them off in their sleeper?

. . . They are leaving . . . They have left! . . .

Ah! If only those we no longer wanted were the only ones stolen from us!

After having suffered twenty-four hours with a continual gnawing pain, what was this peace, this softness, a kind of indifference to what she had thought to be her drama?

Balance—a talent one must not lose! N. fought against love all night. Did she kill it? Did it kill her? Or was it only a truce, a truce that enables us to grant things only as much importance as they deserve.

She even felt capable of never seeing them again—or of seeing them. Let them get intensely involved or have as much fun as they can!

Which one will destroy the other? To no longer be the buffer between these two destructive, devastating principles. To prevent L. from destroying M., or M. from destroying L.? The *match* is equal. Place your bets, *Mesdames!* You can't waltz as a threesome. Other dances need to be invented.

There was now no more room for N. within this couple now united, disappearing like a sinking stone. N. closed in on herself, and their ripples got wider and wider and then—were gone.

She no longer had in her the concentration of strength, the strength of irresistible acts that pave the way for a justification.

Her indifference no longer reeked of any sacrifice. And what good is paradise if we don't risk losing it? And what good is paradise lost—or found? Or a paradise that turned out not to have been a paradise after all? To hit rock bottom, to know the last word from our pride, from our bitter wounds:

"I don't want anything that is not mine. But what isn't mine if I know how to take it? I only want what can be mine and mine alone!

PART THREE

N. Takes Up Her Travel Diaries Again

N. Takes Up Her
Travel Diaries Again

N. takes up her travel diaries.

They mark the path traveled between the creation of a feeling and its destruction.

Espoir et désespoir, that is, hope and despair, are nearly the same word—the word and its reply, its prolonged echo!

~

In this very place, eight months ago, I was imagining my love for M.

Our affair ensued—an affair that was nothing more than a series of infidelities.

The latest and most devastating one pushes me back into this loneliness that I will escape only by forgetting her or loving her all the more. This inner drama folds and unfolds in me. I see our film again in slow motion as a series of episodes—all those scenes flickering between me and the stars. Mirages of intimacy . . . café windows come between me and this tideless sea that washes nothing up, carries nothing away.

I shall light all the little pink candles she used to give me for my nightly departures from her home, and I shall make new constellations with them—to climb the celestial steps of her rickety staircase once more!

I have come so far from the pride that made me say: "I only want what can be mine and mine alone!"

With the help of loneliness, I will turn what little I have left of M. into a great love—a love neither she nor I would ever want—and besides, true love should be pure loss!

~

All intensity is paid in the ready cash of misfortune.

We have spent our energy, far above our credit—let us face our debts, those of us who have mishandled and squandered our riches. Regret is the piety of the miser ruined by his prodigal child! Dare we admit our poverty?

Like a pauper, I lurk about the garishly lit hotel corridors, I slip out into the night, I avoid everyone who could rescue me, I isolate myself and hopelessly do private battle with this hostile feeling that slips through my slumber and wakes me in tears.

I suffer as fully, as purely as if this love had been a true love, blessed with years of happiness, whose enchantment has only just now left me!

I allowed myself to become rashly enmeshed in a web of events I can no longer escape. . . .

It is here that I invented this love; it is here that I miss it. . . .

Regret . . .

I miss your body, its magnificent pleasures, its long vibrations like mine, those nights when you murmured: "If women only knew, if they only knew!"

I miss our outings to meet exceptional people, whose genius we unleashed. . . . And the similar way we reacted. . . . Chance taxi rides when we were so carried away there was no more room for fear. . . . Your carriage entrance where the street lamp shone. . . . Returning home under a light rain . . . and the dim light of the courtyard. . . . Your key and its snaky silver chain you took off. . . . The sound of water when you were getting ready. . . . Cold suppers and glasses of fresh water—before you fell asleep until lunchtime, just as the second lunch was brought in on a double plate warmer by the chauffeur.

I miss our bedside lunches, and our shyness, and your fondness for chicken stuffing. . . . Our rest and naps afterward. . . . Your torso dressed in a white cloud, your legs in blue. . . . The outline of your legs on the bedspread follows a dream path. . . . As long as they do not cross or uncross, or one of them comes uncovered: "If women only knew, if they only knew!"

I miss having boutonnieres to send you, cigarettes to bring to you, pocket money to lend you, opportunities to satisfy you in the depths of your being!

I miss the evenings when you were drunk, and I helped you undress . . . after waiting for you in your echoing bedroom, where the steps of all the other tenants returning home reverberated, before I heard your steps. And the stories you told me behind closed doors in the smoke-filled night . . . Your demands and your kind words, all the more charming for being full of mistakes! And your accent, which intensifies the "r": "Mor-r-r-e! Mor-r-r-e!"

I miss the late afternoons when our "association" was doing good work to the detriment of my good little heart—suffering for the sake of the Cause . . . when I watched—with the terrifying reality of a veroscope[63]— your lips moving toward another's.

I miss every morning when I arrived before you awoke . . . I peeked in the door and saw your curly head on the pillow, your body nestled beneath the sheets making a curve where I joined you—and pretended never to have left you. You awoke so softly, nothing hurried you, you murmured a few unintelligible words, a few syllables of a dream . . . then your hand reached out as if to ask for your lighter and the first cigarette: *"Bonjour, mon amour."*

I miss the hour of your manicure, when I watched your toenails attaining perfection under the clippers and nail file, and when you asked me to write for you, your hands otherwise engaged in the blue-tinged water. . . .

And when your hairdresser would come . . . your hair would smell like a meadow afterward . . . then the drone of the electric hairdryer and the rebellious part to redo. A gray hair . . . the first to be pulled out . . . and you give it to me—to eat—on the sly!

I miss the days when you planned to meet me at a certain time and yet were surprised to find me still there when you returned. Then you turned right around and left to have dinner with friends who had organized a whole evening—leaving mine disorganized.

I miss your domineering look on ultrafeminine days when you called for your most beautiful blouse with the large initials, your best tailored

---

63. A veroscope is a medical instrument used in surgery to provide an endo-scopic view of tissue layers beneath the skin.

jacket, your cleanest hat, and your red choker, then decided against going out after all, and you went back to bed giving orders to let no one in. . . . And your paleness that was more pronounced in the evening. . . . And your blood that I tasted . . . I want to die as I lived, between your thighs. "Only one woman before me has ever managed to leave her mark on you!" How many had taken you and how few possessed you!

I still miss that last night when, having taken off the ring I gave you so that you could put on L.'s wedding ring, you put it back on hastily as you returned to my side. . . . And later on that night, its emerald pressed into your hand clenched in mine—your hand saying farewell to mine at the height of its joy, as if the two would never meet again! My comrade in love, does that hand still wear both rings?

I miss everything I did not have. I miss everything I did have. And everything I shall have no longer? And this life, too alive, that we shall have to bury. . . .

I miss everything, everything, everything. . . .

I miss you, and I miss us. Never was anyone so passionately gifted for living as you—except for me. . . . You! Me! . . .

I'm going to the countryside, to the middle of nowhere. You're going toward love.

Which of us will return to that passionate tenderness that was ours?

∼

But why have regrets if I can find it again, imagine it, feel it once more? What good is having lived this with you if I cannot revive you?

In the olive orchard, the leaves reflect the two colors of your eyes.

Your eyes belong to whoever knows how to see them, the nostrils of your sharp nose to those who know how to breathe them in, even at a distance. And your mouth and your body and the mouth of your body belong to those who know how to wrest them from the invisible.

From near and afar I know how to love your beauty, and your legs that bring you and take you away. And your feet that make the earth beneath them important and light.

We must not attach a sense of possession to beauty: understanding is possession enough and possession, belonging.

But generalizations tell us nothing. Let us say something: the word "beauty" says nothing because it is not individualized. We need to bring out the images behind our eyelids, pay tribute to what we hold inside, and illuminate the page with it.

Correspondence

I come back to read my correspondence under the stout and sickly olive trees.

A telegram from them jars me into realizing that my solitude is still so filled with her—yet I hadn't even noticed it yet.

"We hope that your trip goes as well as ours. All our best. Affectionately, L.-M."

A letter the next day confirmed this unfortunate realization. It was a letter written in both their handwriting, a letter of an established couple if there ever was one:

> Darling, M. loves the countryside, M. loves the house, M. loves everything. She is in a state of grace . . .
>
> Me too.
>
> I slept five or six hours last night without any medication.
>
> We are feeling calmer, and we think often of you . . . Write to us—we love you so tenderly. You are on an altar where we are burning candles. My sweet darling, I am turbulent, like the sea here before us.
>
> M. is smoking less and is winning over everyone here. Your L.
>
> Darling, I am so glad to think that the Newly Miserable Woman is with you—for you and for her. I hope that your trip was delightful!

As for me, I am thoroughly charmed by this place. Here I am
regaining my youth and my past hopes, more and more. L. is
marvelous. I am no longer depressed. You know, I was suffering
and hated autumn because, back where I am from, there is a house
and my mother, both of whom I love, and autumn. But all that
feels distant today. I have rediscovered so much here and, more
and more, I dare say that I am happy. I no longer am afraid to say
it. As for the future—it belongs to me and my love. I have so
much happiness inside that I feel you shall have it too. Write me
and tell me everything that you are doing—will you dare? Be well.
Tenderly yours, M.

I did not write back because I didn't want to admit that I was alone—
and tell them to what extent.

They continued even more beautifully:

I put the photo of your beautiful face in M.'s room. So
you are soaring above our bodies in the golden veils of the
sun—in the foggy gray of the mist—and in the shadows of
the night.

We have no maid, it's quite distressing, but M. is so kind
and laughs all the time. She loves *everything*, maybe even me. She
chants and enchants—and you, and you, and you? L.

Darling, you really are not outdoing yourself with epistolary
charms—it isn't nice not to write us. I must protest and would
like to have news of your precious health. I am in a state of
crescendo-appassionata, the music of all the great masters is within
me, and I dare create music that is very sweet and very profound.
Do please write. Yours, M.

To this score of love, this duo in two parts that made my feelings of
loneliness even worse, I telegraphed:

In order to respond, I am waiting for each of you to write separately on her usual paper.

At this, there was a fresh joint outpouring:

You will have this red paper once again—fiery emotions and the memory of L. as she was before. L. the same as she was, L. back for good. Only M. will write on the coveted blue paper. You can't mix the two in order to have pure happiness. So what will you do with me, my little flax flower?

M. runs in the peaceful countryside; and life goes on, and I will bring her back to you. Let's rid ourselves of our—what? Our sadness—here and there—this way and that—until it is all gone! We mustn't have any more of it. I no longer want to dread sinking into myself . . . My darling, I send kisses—feel my heart beating very hard. Your L.

We searched for your footprints on the beautiful beach yesterday.

Then M.:

. . . And as . . . L. says . . . we looked for your footprints, but we could no longer find them.

I looked for love and I found it . . . love looked for me, and found me . . .

You are too lazy. Go ahead and write me and then I will write back on the blue paper—don't see red!

I am not nosy, but I would very much like to know if N. did what she was supposed to with the Newly Miserable Woman.

What does it matter
It is an
emergency exit
For love.

Yours, darling. M.

M. is so sure of me, of herself, of everything! While I am alone and patient. She always thinks that everyone will love her forever—but no one loves forever!

Don't be so arrogant or triumphant—you have no idea what love has in store for you. Let's be humble and take each other's hand, like blind children led by love.

Cast Out of the Realm of Feelings

All our feelings seem blind, too—they are born from a need for blindness.

To be ripped away from a feeling, from a misunderstanding, from the warmth of an intimacy, is to be thrown back into reality. We cry from the cold and the separation like a newborn—waiting to find our balance, our own strength, our independence, our health, a life of our own.

In the meantime, the life that you led me into goes to my head. And I bump up against your absence—until a star of sheer pain, bursting between my eyes, dawns on me as a new vision.

The saying by Baltasar Gracián takes on an even deeper meaning: "Avoid those who are unhappy."

By saving L. ("N. is my savior," she kept saying this to everyone, even to those who weren't interested), I took on her suffering for her. As with a blood transfusion, there was a spiritual substitution. Wanting to alleviate another person's distress, the strong—who are not quite strong enough—run the risk of being overwhelmed by it instead.

People who "sympathize" with suffering and anxiety, who "share" your pain, are at times more sincere and foolhardy than they themselves realize.

I didn't ask for what happened to me—but my subconscious, being in charge of my soul's evolution, certainly did. In the immaterial world—and even in the material world—our ability to help others depends on the extent to which we are spiritual.

No, I'm not sad that L. is happy at my expense—but I am unhappy that I am unhappy on account of *her* misfortune.

I knew that it was dangerous to rescue someone who appeared to be drowning—but how could I help it? And how would I be worthy of being an example for you if my courage hadn't been strong enough in the first place to carry you like a cross?

Rise, my soul, either to belittle them or compel them to rise to the occasion.

Or to mock them with unbearable generosity?

Or simply to cry out to them: How you have hurt me with the happiness you owe me!

Is there nothing to do to counter this state of being overwhelmed, of obsession? Is there no cure?

Some turn to prayer and become religious, others turn to drugs or to debauchery. I remain merciless with myself. No escape hatch seems acceptable to me. I constantly have to face the enemy. What happened to justify such despondency? Is there anything new or surprising about what is happening to me? As someone who has so little faith in the tenderness of others, do I even have the right to feel disappointment?

In any case, being disappointed already shows a profound lack of discernment.

Obsessions

One day, there will doubtless be an exact science that will measure and calibrate our capabilities, our reflexes, give us the means to handle ourselves more precisely. In the meantime, while we await the fine tuning of our human machine, our heart is beating too fast . . . and it wears down in place, so that we are unable to travel the road we have left . . .

We say all too often: "This noble old man with a generous heart"— but we should have noticed that had he been noble or generous, he would have spent both, well before reaching old age.

I am indeed the third one, dispossessed: a case study, and everywhere I look, I see happy couples, tender and faithful relationships.

Like our Indian chiefs, I drink from a bitter cup without flinching . . .

All the beings we love
Are vessels full of gall which we drink with our eyes closed . . .[64]

Even my "forever friend," my Dearest Friend who counted on me to travel to Algeria, and for whom I sacrificed being with M. and L. for a whole month—and perhaps forever—sent another telegram:

---

64. "Baudelaire, *Poèmes divers*, 'Tous imberbes alors . . . ,' 75–76." Barney, *Amants féminins*, 109n43. The English text is from *The Complete Verse of Baudelaire*, trans. Francis Scarfe (London: Anvil Press Poetry Ltd., 1986), 325.

My friend is sick, need to stay here, can't do the planned trip,
regrets, love.

And if I were sick, would they come running??
Our ordinary body receives all possible devotion, but what friendship
would dare to approach, aid, care for our psychic disasters, these strange
infections contracted by our spirit, doomed to all sorts of nameless pain?

> At night, two rats gnaw
> My heart and my mind
> Every day, two pigeons
> Turn into vultures.

We Enter the Sad Phase of
"She Did This to Me, She Did That to Me"

The Woman I Loved the Most also wrote to me:[65]

For once I regret to say that your patchwork of humans has let
you down—whether it be a deficit, unemployment, or a strike.
You are suffering from depression—suffer from exercise instead!
We could go to Barbizon to spend the last week of October
riding horses and playing golf. I got a letter from L. but I thought
it was useless to respond. She tells me: "I am hurting, you are
hurting, she is hurting . . ."One would think she is a sixteen-year-
old sales clerk! She insidiously goes on: "I fought back: love is a
tricky God,[66] and I feel that the flower N. gave me makes me tipsy
and that this flower will stay with me. And then? I feel that when
N. will summon us back, we won't have the strength to do so. She
deserves better, she deserves everything . . . And how can I be
constantly torn apart like this!" After eighteen years of peace, she
should at least aspire to it now! What is annoying is that she feels

---

65. Rapazzini details the start of the friendship and love affair between Liane
de Pougy and Elisabeth de Gramont in his biography of the latter. He also
describes the end of the friendship, which must not have happened yet when
de Gramont sent this letter. See Rapazzini, *Elisabeth de Gramont*, 390–92.

66. Author's note: But I refuse to believe that God is a boor. [Barney's actual
footnote.]

the need to write this to everyone. Consider yourself better off without them. It's not enough to know that you were cheated on—you must also enjoy it!

Why do they all seem to feel the need to be right?
Seeing L.'s indiscretion, childishness, and duplicity, I let go of all restraint and wrote dangerously to M., almost certain that she would show my letter to L. Was this again to speed up events leading to the inevitable crisis? A last chance? A chance for what?

Can I write to you as if I were lying beside you in your bedroom, where only the birds of paradise on the paper can hear us?
     If you have not found my footprints again, it is—probably— that I did not "brand you as your master." All the same your voice haunts me: "If women knew, if they knew!" Do they know today?
     And why would it matter to me if you write on your blue paper once more, when there is no longer trace of you on the page? Isn't that true? You told me that "the race ahead of us is long," but I am at the end of my rope and even at the end of you!
     After all your letters, I don't know what else to think! Everything is written as "we"—we—(all the two of you need now is a child!). What can I possibly conclude?
     "Only silence is great, everything else is weakness."[67] Let's be weak!
     So will I not be spared the mistakes of love? Will you really be so tactless as to write me like this! You must be under some sort of influence—or else you're sadistic—or your unconscious is holding something against me? Or wants to get even? (You have written me more than once: "Why don't I love you instead of L.?") If I don't like to see the two of you separated, at least I can love both of you separately—my heart's compartmentalizing

------

67. "A. de Vigny, *Les Destinées,* 'La mort du loup,' III, 78." Barney, *Amants féminins,* 111n45. My translation.

function anticipated it. It's beyond me to be jealous of a relationship that I brought about. And how can I blame you for a preference that was mine on both counts? I see L. again, when I loved her the way you do now. Slender and urbane like strong women at their peak, she had developed the habit—in order to excuse her physical daintiness—of swearing, so that men would be more at ease. A person couldn't sleep with an angel that hadn't fallen in some way: with L., it was her swearing!

I was exalted, carried away—just as I was when I was turning twenty—just as you must be now. The first time she told me (when she set a date with me on the same red paper used for writing your latest joint letter): "You will love only me—don't forget that I am very jealous." I wanted to save her from men, just as you want to console her over a man. But perhaps we have no inkling of what true misfortune is? Here's an example: L. went from eighteen years of marriage, of luxurious and pleasant chivalry, eighteen years of perfect devotion, to the delights of a shared love, just as someone can go easily from the ground to the mezzanine, and then from an apartment on the second floor to the landing on a roof-garden—and I'm the "lift-boy": up, up!

And to say that it wasn't her mouth but rather her misfortune that seduced you: an inaccurate diagnosis!

You are lucky that you have not evolved to where I am. I am the person who loves you, who loved you, and now I have to watch the two of you again, reliving—because of me and without me—our youth! All the while I am walking alone on this sad Mediterranean beach, no sign of footprints either, searching for Shelley perhaps washed up on shore, full of salt water, who on his funeral pyre is said to have taken on all the colors of the shipwrecked wood. Legend has it that his heart wouldn't burn— a lesson to remember!

By the way, R. has telegraphed to say that she won't be joining me, and I will be returning to Paris by myself at the end of the month. Send me a telegram with your plans. I need to spend time at Barbizon at the end of October, and then I should be home for good.

You "went looking for love" and you "found it." "Love" "went looking for" you and "found" you.

But I thought that I had found something even more precious than love itself, something so dear to me, even with its heavy burdens, more precious even than the moments where it "returns to the shadows" (that's how you put it), where first of all there is joy—and the habit of joy—and then the joy of the habitual—and then the habit of the habitual—and then tiring of the habit—and then the tiring of the tiring. You should be wary, too, of the *decrescendo appassionata*.

I thought that I had found something without traps, without a name, without vows, for one of my kind. Couples bore me, and I have always hated couples—even when I was part of one. Couples are obsessed with clichés, repetition, rings (why not a ring in your nose, while you are at it!). Couples look too much like the animals entering Noah's ark II by II. There they lose all shame and all nobility. They were the first bourgeois!

Fortunately, some of them come back to their senses; they return to their mystery of their own accord. Others become pets: domesticated.

What has become of the winged beast, the beautiful animal of prey that you were? Not a woman, but a being, not Minna-Wilfred, but Seraphita/Seraphitus.[68]

Will you answer? Or have you reached the point where you no longer even understand yourself? I am the only one who can talk to you in your own language, and love you as you are. I am the one who has not been apart from you for months, not even in my dreams or my thoughts. How to prolong you?

~

68. Balzac's novel *Séraphîta* (published in 1834–35) features the androgynous character Séraphitüs-Séraphîta (S-S), who provokes love from Wilfred, a man who believes S-S to be a woman, and Minna, a woman who believes S-S to be a man.

And now for L. Let us galvanize this old impulse of the heart with some remorse, to make her happiness even more exquisite.

I began my letter with a symbolic frontispiece made from our initials and their evolution—punctuation being of exacting importance here.

N-M   L, N, M   N-L-M   L-M, N   L-M

To make my letter to L. look longer and more informative than my letter to M., I stuffed the envelope with a postcard album, with images from the place in the south where they had planned to go, places I had talked them out of in favor of the Côtes-du-Nord.[69] It was very difficult for me to fill up the entire front page left blank for correspondence. To be honest, my feelings had run dry. So I went to get news of her from one of her old friends whom I had run into in Saint-Tropez. This friend complained and bemoaned the fact that L. was still giving a misconstrued interpretation about the disappearance of a certain necklace. So in my letter I mentioned this to L. as an aside, to get her good and angry for awhile—which happens every single time I criticize her or when I stand up to her. I added that the friend in question seemed to have very beautiful, honest eyes and that I was starting to be able to tell a thief by her eyes. (Wasn't I the one who figured out that the chambermaid in Ouchy was a thief, well before she confessed?)

I dated my letter from prison cell 144 and sent both this decoy and the letter to M. at the same time.

Almost immediately, I received a wire from M.:

Leaving tomorrow to visit the entire Vendée, and then we will go take care of my inheritance.

And the next day, a short note from M., a cold letter of friendship, a friendship that has lost all meaning. My fellow partner in love betrayed me at the first provocation, or even without provocation, with useless lies in favor of the couple, to protect key interests of the community.

---

69. This refers to Côtes d'Armor, near St. Malo in Brittany.

And then this letter from L.:

So I have eyes like a thief? Me! Me!! Me!!! I took nothing from you, because you did not own her. She always said that to me. She is still saying it today. And this is all written down, *everything!* *everything!!* *everything!!!*

But even if everything was written down, she didn't refer to what was written. If she gets that upset, it is because she wants to!

Then a feeling of guilt passed over me. Maybe I was wrong . . . I wanted to be wrong. I telegraphed back straightaway saying that I was sorry she thought I meant that she had a thief's eyes, that I was writing about the maid, and that this kind of misunderstanding shouldn't come between us.

They had someone else answer me: "Those women have left."

"If you lie, you don't exist." My little ones, my teensy little ones, my itsy bitsy ones, you would disappear if you did that![70]

---

70. Author's note: N. had jotted down and then erased underneath this: "What a soap opera to explain what it took for me to finally smile again." [Barney's actual footnote].

A Trip on Her Own,
or The Third One without Plan

I returned to Paris. It was difficult for me to return, in short autumnal stages.

Nothing drew me back there; nothing was waiting for me there—or anywhere else either.

I went past some Roman amphitheater, remains of the Roman occupation. Why have a place and a public show, a bloodbath of cruelty, I wondered. Does it diminish in any way an individual's cruelty?

At dusk I arrived at the next hotel, where I spent the night with my various selves, not exactly alone—with the Bible, and with "The Honest Whore" by Decker that the Newly Miserable Woman had sent me, with this passage underlined:

> Strumpets like cheating gamesters will not win at first
> These are but baits, to draw him in
> To abandon her; the harlot does undo him,
> She has bewitched him, robbed him of his shape,
> Turned him into a beast, his reason lost.[71]

---

71. The original English quotation is from Thomas Dekker's (1572–1652) play "The Honest Whore." Barney translated this passage into French alongside the original English passage: "Les putains comme tricheurs au jeu ne gagnent pas de suite. / Ce ne sont qu'appeaux pour attirer à elles— / Elles prient qu'on les

Thanks to L.'s ugly machinations, I began tearing down her declining beauty—by unleashing my worst self against her:

How dangerous it is to have so much beauty to lose!

How to forgive her for this ache in my mind—that I hold against her . . . this ache. . . . this ache!

L., protect me from L., protect me from these thoughts! You no longer fear folding in on yourself? Where is the loyalty that was so attractive to M.!

L. hurts me with L.

Books, like people, only come to me with certain passages that appeal to me directly.

The word "Italy," spoken by a passerby, was like a stab in the back.

Chopped into bits, our feelings were still twitching, even though they were deprived of the very thing that gave them life.

. . . Did your loyalty bother her in the end? She used it to get you undressed, and then she suppressed it—just as you can blow out a candle before going to bed! That's just how she is. And didn't M. tell me: "I will erase everything—even the memory of you"? It's true that, at the time, she was referring to the Woman I Loved the Most—and not L. Indeed, M. took it upon herself to win her over after L.!

I had correctly imagined that L.'s monopolizing of M. would successfully win her over, with L. being so well versed in this kind of thing: the weaker of the two always dominates.

It is less painful for me to doubt your friendship than your character. But the quality of love is only recognizable by what it illuminates. And the quality of love is judged not only by how the loved one is treated but also by how others are treated.

And has there been any gracious or grand gesture from the two of them since they have been together?

Even so, I was receptive, attentive, open, and delicate.

---

abandonne / Pour mieux ensorceler, pour lui voler sa raison, / Changer sa forme en brute méconnaissable . . . !" The editors of the French edition note that Barney's French translation is very liberal and that the passage is in fact two different quotations from the play merged together (Barney, *Amants féminins*, 115n48).

This is how a couple destroys everything around it—and then destroys itself!

"We can judge them, not by how they love, but by how they are when they no longer love!"

~

M. loves L., L. loves M., M. does not love N. N., this friend "in her thoughts" she neglects.

So why are they now treating me as an opponent—and a dangerous one at that, since they are lying to me.

Nothing has changed—so why all this mystery, these flights, these deceptive telegrams . . . ? Yes, M. sympathizes with all suffering—except the suffering she causes. And L. is only able to measure her happiness in proportion to the amount of pain she causes. Or were they simply afraid that I would chase them? The horn of don Ruy Gomez?[72] Or, like Shylock, afraid that I would demand my "pound of flesh"? What a lack of insight about me, what a lack of consideration! Everything has thus returned to traditional roles, despite my efforts. Needing an opponent, the lovers prompt me by giving me my lines—and then conspire against me!

How could I possibly get in their way? It's unlikely that I would go farther than Barbizon, since I hate the countryside. They know how flexible I can be—too flexible in fact—having my soul as my only absolute. I can give myself over completely and withdraw completely—make something out of nothing, and make nothing out of something!

What did they think?

What if I had refused L.'s "sacrifice" each time? How much harder would it be to refuse it now? What then? Then—there is something else!

There is this deserted countryside, cradled by mountains, near the city of Le Puy-en-Velay, with a few beasts of burden and nothing more.

---

72. "This is an allusion to the play *Hernani* by Victor Hugo, in which Don Ruy Gomez gives a horn back to Hernani that Hernani had originally given to him, making the old man master over his life when the horn would sound. As for Shylock, he is a character in Shakespeare's *The Merchant of Venice*." Barney, *Amants féminins*, 117n49.

Malthus probably never came here.[73] Why should it be surprising that the most intelligent people favor depopulation, since animals are less destructive than humans and nature is nobler than animals?

∿

I gain open waters, but I feel the harpoon tearing my side.

The memory floats on the lightest of white wines, dances on violin strings, and is crushed under the scales of the player piano. In Vichy, I think about how she spent last summer here with S.S. . . . Was she then how she is now with L.? Or not?

Beings are rarely different from what they really are; the same situations cause them to be the same. If being unfaithful only provides the opportunity to refresh your feelings but not to reinvent yourself, then being unfaithful loses its greatest value. If we want to see a change, shouldn't it apply to ourselves first and foremost?

I don't expect anything different from L., no more so than from a doll with moveable joints. Those who choose a direction are in control of themselves—and of others. But in control of what? Wasn't she sufficiently warned? But she insists on winning, not on maturing. Besides, L. knows her audience—made up of lovers—just like a diva who always sings the same songs, sure of her old repertoire, thrilled to enjoy the same success!

∿

Why upset them and make them afraid—why give them what they fear— why chase after them, just like a real *opera buffa*? To turn toward the Vendée and Bordeaux? Spy on them at night through the windows of the "house of betrayal"? Show up during their walk, coming out of the fog? Burst out laughing, and then disappear in a whirl of dead leaves? Go

---

73. Thomas Robert Malthus (1766–1834) was an English demographer who wrote about the economics of overpopulation, believing that population growth would always outpace food production. Barney was clearly familiar with Malthus's theories, and she writes about the dangers of overpopulation in her *Pensées d'une Amazone*.

up the stairs stealthily behind them, like a traveler who can do anything because of her immateriality? Slip between them in the bed of betrayal? It will be my kiss and her mouth. "I am the one who makes love increase." There is something to this effect in Dante, which M. probably knows:

Ecco qui crescera i nostri amori.[74]

~

It's too bad that the most attractive women discourage any permanence. A marvelous sensation machine, M. is not good at directing the action. She ruins everything—just like I do; she sabotages both the love and the beautiful heartbreak that we would like to owe her!

~

My ladies, you inspire beautiful feelings that you then destroy. And you are living without learning how to live . . . Learning to live, knowing how to live—the word has replaced the deed.

Epicurus is the only philosopher who never had a good disciple: that is because living well requires an awareness of every moment.

~

I was about to make a discovery—but the sensuality that pushes us into such adventures taints any benefit we might attain.[75]

~

---

74. "Here Barney cites a verse from memory, taken from Dante's *Divine Comedy*, 'Ecco chi crescerà li nostri amori.'" Barney, *Amants féminins*, 118n50. A translation of this line is "How this one will augment Our lives!" Dante Alighieri, *Heaven*, canto 5, in *The Divine Comedy*, trans. Clive James (New York: Liveright, 2013).

75. Barney compiled a list comprising many of her love relationships, classifying them into three categories: *liaisons*, *demi-liaisons*, and *aventures*. Whereas de Gramont, Brooks, and de Pougy are considered *liaisons*, Mimi Franchetti is listed as an *aventure*. Rapazzini, *Elisabeth de Gramont*, 490–91. For this reason, it is especially important to keep the word "adventure" in the translation.

What do I have left from the adventures I took part in? M. with love that does not reach out!

This *lock-out* worried me. This love did not last long outside—it didn't reveal enough of me . . .

Few beings express who they are through their passion. Few find the best use of themselves. Saint Theresa is quite fortunate!

∿

The principle of least effort doesn't mean loving someone like ourselves.

Here is a little saying for children who don't behave: the lover whose rudeness we tolerate toward others will wind up being just as rude to us. Your bad deeds take on a life of their own and turn against you.

What an obsession—having to destroy someone else in order to get proof of your love. L. no doubt said to herself: "How can I increase my prestige? By stealing what was given to me."

The wounds to our pride only heal when we hurt someone else! But I have no pride! I have only love, a love whose unhealthy part—now corroding and deteriorating—comes from them!

∿

It's too bad that they ended the game; it was a healthy sport—and their relationship's best chance of lasting.

> . . . gestures
> That lovers invent so as to kill off love.[76]

If they cling together so tightly, is it perhaps because they are afraid to lose one another, or else afraid to put an end to their loneliness? Or is it

---

76. "This is an incomplete quotation of two verses from the poem 'Anne' by Paul Valéry in *Album de vers anciens* (*strange* gestures / That lovers invent . . .)." Barney, *Amants féminins*, 120n51. The English text is from Paul Valéry, *Collected Works of Paul Valéry*, volume 1, *Poems*, trans. David Paul (Princeton: Princeton University Press, 1971), 51.

because they become so close that they forget to pay attention to each other, since they belong to each other.

Lovers become immune to their feelings: only the jealous lover owns her joy!

~

Perhaps I am not jealous enough: but can I envy the happiness that I create?

~

Why is it that people cannot engage in any amorous exchange without being engulfed by it? It is undoubtedly left over from the feeling of the Absolute!

~

L. always demands more, I always less, than we had to give. So they take the little bit I had, giving L. what wasn't anyone's to give!

~

And even if I had M. to myself, would I be satisfied, like L. is?

~

Something that makes me so discontented could in no way make me happy.

~

When I am alone with someone, I think of those that I am not with.

My body and mind are never in the same place—they take separate vacations!

And if I am constantly searching for joy, that's because it is the only thing that makes me whole.

The rest of the time—and there is so much leftover time—I want what I don't want—and I don't want what I want!

~

Every time Pharaoh freed the Israelites, just when they were leaving, he would prepare all the war chariots, all his best units, gathering all his power to bring them back! (True, this hesitation to let go of his fury finally ended badly in the Red Sea!)

∾

In the end, L. and M. are right . . .

> So sleep on, lovers. Meanwhile, all around,
> A world careless of things delicate
> Bangs and thumps or drowses in wickedness
> Without the brains to be jealous of you. (Verlaine)[77]

The thought of them together soothes me—soothes me to sleep!
    L. has her sleep again—soon that is all that she will have!

∾

I just translated this passage by Milton, following the sound of this mechanical movement that unwinds in me, like the movement of a memory with a certain cadence. I loved it when I was a child:

> Adieu, champs bienheureux de la béatitude,
> Salut, monde infernal, enfer le plus profond,
> Reçois ton possesseur nouveau—un qui t'apporte
> Un esprit que le temps ni l'espace ne changent.
> L'esprit seul est le Lieu—seul, en lui-même, obtient
> Un ciel de son enfer—un enfer de son ciel,
> Et qu'importe où . . . si moi je suis encore le même
> Et tel que je dois être . . .

---

77. "Verlaine, *Parallèlement*, 'Ces passions que seuls nomment encore amour.'" Barney, *Amants féminins*, 121n52. The English text is from Paul Verlaine, *Selected Poems*, trans. Martin Sorrell (New York: Oxford University Press, 1999), 198.

Farewell, happy fields,
Where joy for ever dwells! Hail, horrors! hail,
Infernal World! And thou, profoundest Hell,
Receive thy new possessor—one who brings
A mind not to be changed by place or time.
The mind is its own place, and in itself
Can make a Heaven of Hell, a Hell of Heaven
What matter where, if I be still the same,
And what should I be [. . .]⁷⁸

Are we not truly masters of our minds—and foremen of their image factories?⁷⁹ Let's work to perfect them. The mass-produced truths need to be sorted out, to be perfected. They deserve the right to circulate freely.

---

78. "Milton, *Paradise Lost*, book 1, lines 249–57. These lines are pronounced by Satan when he leaves Heaven and sees Hell for the first time." Barney, *Amants féminins*, 121n53. The English text is from John Milton, *Paradise Lost*, ed. John A. Himes (Dover, 2005), 9. Barney's French is included here with the English to emphasize her status as a bilingual writer and as a translator herself. Indeed, Paul Valéry asked her to translate a number of his works into English. With Ezra Pound's assistance, her translation of "An Evening with M. Teste" was published in *Dial* (1922). Rodriguez, *Wild Heart*, 232, 243.

79. There are puns that are inevitably lost in the translation. Here, she plays on the similarity of *maître* and *contremaître*.

In Love with Water

The stopover tonight will be the hotel where all three of us stayed on our way back from Switzerland . . .

I will bathe myself in the memory of her veins, in the warmth running from her veins. That enormous bathroom—already famous—sparkling with porcelain, electricity, mirrors, and the art of erotic plumbing—because that was where M. had called me to come look at her veins. They were flowing from everywhere near the surface of her skin and on surface of the water. I will bathe myself in the memory of her veins—in water running as warm as her veins.

When she was marveling at these achievements in the art of erotic plumbing, L. thought that these wonderful vertical showers could replace carnal pleasures if need be . . . M. wasn't so sure.

I remained silent, proud of a certainty I've held since childhood, when I discovered the virtues of water, thanks to a faucet in the shape of a swan's head! I celebrated the flowing lover's rhythms that came back to me, in honor of this first meeting:

> I am in love with water
> who purifies me from other beings.
> I lay in the fresh fountains

and open my arms to water.
I love water, whose embrace escapes me
whose kiss brushes against me.
I am in love with water
who fills everything up.
He is so heavy, my clear lover[80]
he is so light!
May his energy console
the brutal, heavy weight of beings.
I am in love with erratic water
he who never changes.
I place myself under his moving body
he who possesses me, yet leaves me more virginal than before.
His insinuations are rapes,
his caress is ever-changing,
he avoids me and still grows more insistent . . .
The flowers of the water know it well,
the flowers of the water are my sisters
everything that taints water
and everything that dies far from it.
Weary from unknown things
from ecstasies that we forget,
from Gods who have an end,
from beliefs that we renounce,
from devotion without faith
from passions that make me cold,
weary from everything that is
and everything that is yet to come
bodies drawing closer

---

80. The masculine-gendered word *amant* is used throughout the text; here, I put it in the masculine, as there is significant emphasis on the pronoun "he" throughout this passage. This could be read, however, as gender neutral or perhaps even interpreted in the feminine.

minds separating
from everything that pulls us apart
or painfully brings us together
I am in love with water
who purifies me of beings . . .[81]

But instead of reaching climax during this aquatic rendezvous, the darkness and the rain forced me to stop before seeing images of M. and her veins. And so I retired to a chaste room without any shutters, with a single bed and just a pitcher of cold water!

. . . Should I stop in Barbizon to sleep, surrounded by this white-and-green gingham checkerboard—this pattern of hope that she nailed above my bed?
    I'm done with this game of checkers, this *"jeu de dames"* . . .[82]

Freedom—Solitude, they make an attractive couple, all the same—and they best adapt to the third one.

But the serpent, cut into pieces, writhes until nightfall . . .

---

81. "A version of this poem appears in the epilogue of the poetry collection entitled *Cinq petits dialogues grecs* (1902), which Barney published under the name Tryphé. Barney has varied the rhythm of the poem here." Barney, *Amants féminins*, 123n54.

82. The play on words of *jeu de dames* here is lost in the translation. While *jeu de dames* means "game of checkers," she is also hinting at its literal meaning of "game between ladies" in the love triangle.

Regaining Balance

My black cat greets me from the window . . .

Once at home, my walls give me a feeling of well-being.

I am told that my second dove has died.

From the entry hall, I see the snake cane that M. had sent me—afterward. It doesn't really affect me much: even dead snakes made into canes lose their symbolic venom.

Letters—more letters from them. So I was right. Just as volcanoes erupt underwater, so too do tense situations erupt in silence. I cannot fully understand the magnitude of this eruption. Nothing makes a feeling turn into resentment faster than when its sustenance has been taken away!

I take my mail upstairs. Among the papers, death announcements. As soon as we turn our back, our friends drop like leaves. They take advantage of a vacation to leave definitively—exploiting this moment meant merely for taking a break by letting themselves die!

$\sim$

Partner, not a word from you? You are betraying our *trust*—this advance of the heart—to join the classic ranks of lovers: "You relinquish yourself when you become part of a couple." And what, pray tell, do you get in return? What kind of self-cure must it be to be a victim of such a spell? It must equal the renunciation demanded by the church. And should I envy you—I who have never had this kind of faith? Even if we have followers, is it because we need them? Let's question this demand that Jehovah seemed to impose on his chosen people. No deceived lover has ever been so unfair and vengeful!

～

Relinquish being the third one? Is it possible?

It's awkward, a miserable *ménage à trois*, a kind of *malheur à trois*—that is to say, a three-way misery: there are too many points of view . . . But what is their happiness worth, if my misery wants no part in it?

～

I open a letter from a young neighbor who has been sending me caresses, kisses, and spelling mistakes for four years. She is again offering me caresses and kisses (who knows what her teeth are like!) along with her love—but I can only accept the love that I offer myself!

Her naivety nonetheless amuses me. She just visited Lac du Bourget and is surprised that this expanse of water has not aged, in spite of Lamartine's verse:

> When I saw you
> Oh clear lake
> I was surprised
> That after all these years
> You water is not cloudy . . .[83]

That's a new way of thinking about it. Why don't we apply it to feelings? Would only the heart be prudent and conventional?

～

A note from a "principled libertine" taunts me:

---

83. My translation.

I am happy that you are in this wonderful place—but less so because you don't have a favorite person there with you. It's like imagining a general without his sword, or a priest without his altar. How can it be that your beautiful friend is detained, so far from you? Granted, L. has certain little ways of doing things. But I just cannot believe that anyone could outdo you in the art of depending on ingenuity! It doesn't matter—sometimes it takes very little to win. You will need to see that!

People have told me that A.'s joke didn't come out in the way I told you. Not "I saw N., the Pope of debauchery," but rather that I must have misunderstood A.'s shrill voice saying, "I saw N., the Pope of Lesbos." So that's that!

And my know-it-all—knowing so little these matters—was the very same woman who had written a complete list of cuckolds in history as a way of giving L. condolences about her marriage. Sooner or later, this know-it-all led me to realize something about M. or L.:

> The only fruit of love that I shall gather
> Tears, which are not for me. . . .[84]

and that this happened to Racine when he was at the École Normale . . .

∿

The Woman I Loved the Most canceled Barbizon, perhaps reluctant to play a role that was beneath her.

∿

In this epidemic of desertions, I regain my balance through an instinct for self-preservation, unencumbered by my closest friends. Have they grown close to me only to make me suffer all the more?

---

84. The editors of the French edition point out that Barney did not correctly remember the quotation (Barney, *Amants féminins*, 126n55). I have provided

To stay in closer contact with them and the suffering that they alone can cause me, I turn off the switch between myself and the outside world.

I flip the switch back on . . . to find myself surrounded by vibrations from everywhere. The nameless woman reclaims her rights—and I am greeted by a witty note and a bouquet of flowers. I am all finished with this hyperbole of the senses, the restrictive nature of exclusive relationships. I put things in order; I put my life back in its place. They should leave it alone!

I go back through this notebook with horror, with embarrassment. I wander in it, just like in some of my dreams—as if completely naked in front of a group of people wearing clothes, who will certainly see me and condemn me for having taken a walk in the nude! I open my last notebook: I catch myself red-handed.[85]

Now I confess everything to the blank pages that follow, to the same confessional where I admitted my sins. This act of contrition is a revelation of myself: the inordinate gesture is the deliverance from an inner crime. But we are punished only for our confessions!

The childish and destructive side of strong emotions—this venom that poisons our entire system—shocks me to my core, as much as it would if it didn't come from me.

---

the quotation here from Jean Racine, *Berenice*, trans. John Masefield (London: W. Heinemann, 1922), 34.

85. This "notebook" appears to be the very book upon which this novel is based.

A Better Epicureanism

I have returned to a better Epicureanism.[86]

The purity of each blank page greets me—it will be the judge, according to a vision more profound than mine. A complicity necessary to my fragile healing establishes itself between myself and me! I open my heart to myself!

Most of us aspire to love, to lose ourselves—others love to find themselves. I don't know which of the two is better—I have felt the exaltation of losing myself—and so much happiness in finding myself again!

I brought an integrity that I didn't always leave with to "this refined diversion that we call love."

Do these games of passion go beyond honesty to the point that we couldn't even pride ourselves on revenge?

So I don't hate L.? I obediently use the tooth powder she got for me.

I get ready for bed—it is always so delicious to go to bed. As long as I feel my leg against the other and my hand in my hand . . .

---

86. Epicurus was an ancient Greek philosopher; Barney expressed an affinity with his philosophy.

And what if M. comes back? It happens—it already happened to me with R.V.[87] and others.

"My God—let me be spared this happiness!"

The state of being *in love* is even less defined than that of being *out of love*. Even when my feelings of attachment were not secure or complete, my feelings of detachment were.

"You won't have me—you brat—you won't have me anymore!"

Near my bed, I see M.'s little compass oscillating, the collection of pink candles in their yellow pot, the pocket knife that is still open, and the box where M. had carved—metal on metal—some word that was less resistant.

Dear Little *Sole Mio*—you needed something clearer than the initial tenderness we shared, something weaker than our amorous friendship.

I hear their duet: "Love is stronger than anything else."

Well, too bad for love!

Even when in love, I have always met tyranny with force. Tyranny is nothing more than fear!

And, indeed, is there anything we dread more than being a slave? Or having the temperament of a slave? And here it is starting all over again?

Your retreat into the shadows doesn't enlighten anyone!

You never can tell what slaves really think—slaves themselves do not know what they think—all their thoughts are in service!

The master's nerves are no longer focused, and so he punishes the victim by constraining him.

Henry James said it best: "There is only one person who is worse than the tyrant: the tyrant's victim!"

Having no one to talk with, no one to stand up to, talking incessantly into an echo. There is no such thing as a good slave, no slave who does nothing more than atone for each action—a good slave does not rebel in a servile way! And why do we insist on making all those in our proximity

---

87. Renée Vivien (1877–1909, pseudonym of Pauline Tarn) was an accomplished poet, and Barney's relationship with her was one of her most important. Karla Jay provides an excellent introduction to her work and life in *The Amazon and the Page*.

become like us? Perhaps it is a kind of fidelity, not to the individual, but rather to stasis itself. If we are capable of reducing all beings in the same way, then we only have one kind to deal with.

Even in sculpture, a couple does not have its own equilibrium. If you take away the support between the two figures, the entire façade collapses.

↝

My dear love, torment of idleness, here I am returning to my autumn gardening.

I collect the dead leaves, leaving a trail of decomposition.

Whose wrist has the softness of my rake's handle?

↝

Tonight I will be the host that everyone dreads seeing arrive[88]
Casting an inevitable shadow in the doorway
I will take my invisible place at the table
Happy, and like a soft and insinuating trouble
You will feel my body slip between the two of you
Near one another, do you sometimes miss me?
Calling me softly with muted anguish,
You will see my provocative look in
Her eyes, and you will hold me in her open arms,
Just like before, I will come to your bed
And it will be my kiss, even if it is her mouth!

Know me: I am not someone who can be chased out of someone's life!

↝

Oh! If only you could return while I am making you larger than life— while your life still beats in me, while my life clings to you, while your face is beneath my eyelids and your veins fill my veins.

Regardless—I am rich keeping you despite having lost you. Do I really need you—to have you?

---

88. This poem appeared in a different location in the manuscript and it was an editorial decision to put it here; I am following the French publication in its placement here.

Three Dialogues between N. and the Newly Miserable Woman

I

_____

The Newly Miserable Woman (N.M.): I just learned something that makes me feel that my affair with T. has run out of steam.[89] It is only a matter of time or convenience before everything falls apart. Every time T. comes home at seven in the morning after a night of drinking, I try to think about my new book so that I don't make a scene. I should love this book above all else.

N.: Yes, after all, your talent is stronger, more important, more enduring . . .

N.M.: Oh, forget about all that! Think—finally—about your own.

N.: But my talent, my art, is living.

N.M.: You're not doing it very well!

N.: Perhaps a bit on purpose. The cards need to be shuffled so as to call out all the trumps.

N.M.: So you judge the game by how passionate it is?

N.: And by the integrity of the players.

N.M.: Everyone has always claimed that it had no place in the game of passion!

N.: I tend to insist on it, often in situations where others aren't used to finding it.

N.M.: And you lose the game! You should be sad about what happens to you, beyond words.

_____

89. N.M. here refers to Djuna Barnes, and T. refers to Thelma Wood.

N.: Women of letters like us are never sad "beyond words."

N.M.: Therein lies our consolation. We know when we aren't loved, but we don't really know when we aren't read!

N.: My principal works have been—alas—of the flesh.

N.M.: Are you incorrigible?

N.: Perhaps, of all the discoveries, love is the most exciting . . . Few can resist this voyage of discovery . . .

N.M.: In the tropics. . . . Aren't the fevers pretty bad there?

N.: Or else they abandon the mission, having seen signs that their companion is not well suited to them.

N.M.: Dostoevsky noted that everything ends in pettiness.

N.: All the better, as this allows us to belong to others!

N.M.: You are relentless. Haven't you ever wanted someone to your-self, just to yourself, everything for yourself—forever?

N.: That's not something I would want—it is the despicable calcula-tion of a miser, and we have no right to it. I have only encountered endur-ing qualities twice in my adventurous forays, when I found two beings who were worthy of being part of my true life.[90]

N.M.: But it seems to me that you often sacrifice your true life to your explorations.

N.: The job has a hold on me.

N.M.: And the risk?

N.: The risk does too.

N.M.: And what if you lost them?

N.: I would only be losing something that wasn't mine!

N.M.: You are hard on them, and on yourself!

N.: It's Epicurean discipline. Isn't it Epicurean to continually attract life, and suffer more and better than others?

N.M.: So, no shelter? You will be constantly looking for opportunities to prove your heroism. You realize that?

N.: I like the exercise of pitting one force against the others.

N.M.: You don't find that your adversaries are equally well armed?

---

90. As noted in the translator's essay, the two enduring relationships alluded to here are with Romaine Brooks and Elisabeth de Gramont.

N.: Actually, yes, I do, because I am handicapped by having more heart.

N.M.: A heart just like mine: a Second Empire heart. It forces you to give endlessly—and give everything: the strong, the true, the warm, the tender, all of your best qualities come into play.

N.: Under a veneer of irony—through innocence!

N.M.: We need to make our virtues unrecognizable. How does it turn out?

N.: I interest people in themselves and in others, more so than in me.

N.M.: For fear of being burdened?

N.: For fear of burdening them, too.

N.M.: You think of happiness as a kind of unemployment—you need to continue moving forward.

N.: Those who make history have a flair for the future: they can see it before others do.

N.M.: But don't they try to talk anyone into it? Have you always led others to good things?

N.: I led them to themselves! You will never make me believe that monopolizing, undermining, captivating, holding onto, and drugging others with yourself is living well or helping others to live.

N.M.: Do you think that our love needs fresh air?

N.: We must free, develop, and push those who fall into our arms toward realizing their potential.

N.M.: So you have never held someone back to help you or for you to help them? You have always tried to guide them toward their future, even if it didn't include you?

N.: We need to try to anticipate their evolution, catch them not where they are, but where they are going! . . . It's only in going backward that we lose them.

N.M.: As in the present situation?

N.: I still don't know about the present situation.

N.M.: To risk losing everything so that nothing escapes you? That is a bad policy—the policy of a depraved king . . . Yes, you go from one end of the battlefield to the other without respite, just to make sure that everything is combat ready, seeing if there is no hope of some plot, some sort of treason against your sovereignty. Knowing that you can count on treachery, you provoke it if you need to! Not even our hereditary and natural enemies, Illness and Death, are enough to make your old solitary heart bleed. The heart is not even aware of its own lifeblood, unless it is flowing! And this heartens your troops? Never any rest. Kings have no right to retreat!

N.: The mind, if you will, is indeed a kind of king who can do nothing without passion.

N.M.: Trapped between spirit and passion is the heart of the eternal victim?

N.: There is no eternal victim.

N.M.: Give me your sword.

N.: Why?

N.M.: To end the fight! Do you have a light?

⌒

N. went into the next room to look for M.'s cigarettes for the Newly Miserable Woman. There should be some left—were there?

Not finding any, she came back holding a powder box with a butterfly on it. One of two different music box tunes play every time the box is opened, impregnating the room with these shrill memory-filled notes.

N.M.: What's that?

N.: A gift from The Woman I Loved the Most. (In a profoundly melancholic state, N. listened to the second song in the cycle:

*need old acquaintance be forgot
or never brought to mind . . .*)[91]

N.M.: The person who gave you that certainly had charm.

N.: Do you think that I don't remember?

Then N. remembered her dream she had the night before, in which her Dearest Friend never returned.

---

91. "This is a popular Scottish song based on the poem attributed to Robert Burns. Barney here has modified it by substituting 'need' for 'should.'" Barney, *Amants féminins*, 135n60. This song is entitled "Auld Lang Syne," which can be translated as "Long Long Ago."

Once the Newly Miserable Woman had left, N. began organizing her papers. She found the letter that hadn't made much of an impression at the beginning of the summer. With a shiver, she remembered the heavy door that had closed between them.

Alone night after night, with Madame B.,[92] N. kept thinking: Should it come as a surprise that her Dearest Friend was gone, that she had gotten emotionally involved in a way that had a hold on her, and that it kept her away, now that N. needed her the most?

On a whim, she wrote:

If I appeared negligent toward you, perhaps it was to make you atone in advance for the pain that you were bound to cause me. Our nerves are the barometers of storms to come. I am now being punished for not weighing in advance the significance of your slightest action. You have a knack for hitting just the right spot, striking us at the very place where we are weak.

Then she discarded these beginnings of a confession, a confession that no one needed. Discipline is the best part of such affection. No need to bother this friend with protests that she no longer wants to hear.

Melancholy overtook her, the melancholy of another person. . . . Her heart, which had been straying, returned to normal under the pressure of this genuine fear . . . and beat like alarm drums with all its might!

Phantom women, will-o'-the-wisps, imaginary sufferings with no rhyme or reason, and which are completely unfounded: the minor key intertwined with a musical theme one can barely hear, for all the combinations and overlayering of notes and rests of different lengths. It should be enough to send us back to plainsong that ends on a major chord.

Caught up with the thrill of making her own music, would she even hear it? Would she even respond? She was beautiful and patient, so she deserved everything. If this is really for the best, if this is what truly makes her happy, then let's join in with the only means we have left: abstinence—and silence!

---

92. Madame Blavatsky is an author, so N. is reading her books. See note 31.

II

First Chill

The Newly Miserable Woman (N.M.): But what will you do when you are old? Not just old from time to time, or old in certain places, but definitively ensconced in old age as in a small cabin that doesn't even have the bare essentials?

N.: And that's what you want to ask someone to share?

N.M.: Well, that's when we need a companion the most. What do other people do? What will you yourself do?

N.: When our hearts become two old maids
   Joined together like the double hearts of the hourglass
   Sifting time from top to bottom,
   Sifting everything that they no longer feel, but dread
   forgetting! . . .[93]

N.M.: As for me, I cling to T. . . . She is as good as any other, why not her instead of someone else? It isn't necessary to grow old or die alone!

N.: And what about when she cheats on you . . . would you know it? Like now . . . ?

N.M.: I will close my eyes . . .

---

93. "This is a quatrain of one of Barney's poems that was published later in the journal *Le Manuscrit autographe*, no. 39, 1932." Barney, *Amants féminins*, 137n62. My translation.

N.: So that she can be there to close them for you? Doesn't it seem equally important to have someone who can open them for you? Everyone, let's all conjugate together:

I close my eyes,
You close my eyes,
We close each other's eyes,
They close each other's eyes . . .

N.M.: You would prefer:

I open my eyes,
You open my eyes,
We open each other's eyes,
They open each other's eyes . . . ?

N.: Even with our eyes open, we don't see that well!

N.M.: That's just it. In your conjugation, no couple would survive. Even in Ecclesiastes, the most bitter of all the bitter chapters in the bitter Bible, it proclaims: "Two are better than one; because they have a good reward for their labour. For if they fall, the one will lift up his fellow: but woe to him that is alone when he falleth; for he hath not another to help him up." And it goes on: "Again, if two lie together, then they have heat: but how can one be warm alone? And if one prevail against him, two shall withstand him; and a threefold cord is not quickly broken."[94]

N.: There are people who would be pleasant to be with our whole lives—but not at the cost of lies, hypocrisy, closed eyes, concessions, or sacrifices.

N.M.: But what if you couldn't keep them any other way?

---

94. Ecclesiastes 4:9–10, 11–12. The editors of the French edition point out that Barney's translation is only an approximation of the actual passage (Barney, *Amants féminins*, 138n63). The English translation here is from the King James Version.

N.: There is no other way.

N.M.: But you can't even keep them that way either, if we look at your life. There is the old proverb: "You can't both run and hold on."

N.: You can't hold on and on either. Let's look around us. Who stays together? Who stays faithful? Husbands leave their wives or sleep on the opposite side of the house. Children leave their parents, and covet their wealth.

N.M.: Parents leave their children—for other children. Nothing is stable in the natural order of things.

N.: Yet we ground our hopes there. People are deluded by their hopes. Every kind of human association disappoints—because we expect more of people than they can possibly give.

N.M.: People who cling and people who let go are by turns the same person; they just switch roles.

N.: In the end, maybe it is nobler and more natural to live alone, despite what Ecclesiastes says.

N.M.: So we are born, only to suffer and die? There are favors to obtain, adjustments, compensations, and arrangements to offer unto unhappiness.

N.: I was once at an antique music collector's where I saw a harpsichord, commissioned by a nobleman, whose lid was delicately painted upon on the orders of a lord. For various reasons, he had wanted himself depicted with the four people dear to him: his mother, his wife, his mistress, and his friend. They were all gathered together and depicted on this part of the lid in perfect harmony among themselves, with each other, and in relation to him: they each had their particular attributes and their appointed place beside him. No one seemed to misunderstand or be jealous. These four relationships were not particularly harmful.

N.M.: But these four necessities seem to be irreconcilable!

N.: I wonder: Did the architect of the heart divide it into four chambers for just this purpose? The right valve of the heart . . .

N.M.: But blood only needs to circulate once to upset this neat arrangement. The heart's coat of arms is quickly turned upside down. The mistress is found drowned in the liver, the wife weighs down on the stomach, the mother barely keeps going, thanks to a safety valve, and the friend reaches the head where he is close to all sorts of thoughts that he'd rather not have known!

~

They continued this dialogue while walking through the Tuileries Garden, and then arrived at Prunier's to have their first lunch of the fall season:

N.: Fresh caviar and celery stalks.

N.M.: Oysters?

N.: No oysters.

N.M.: Are you afraid of them? It appears that F.L. died of them.

N.: I only fear danger when I have an appointment. That's why I always ask for the gentlest horse when I hunt, and I make sure that the taxi driver pays attention when I am in the city.

N.M.: I noticed that you weren't paying attention when you crossed the street just now!

N.: What is the special today?

N.M.: Saddle of hare.

N.: Yes.

N.M.: Poor thing . . .

N.: It's a bit too late to think of that! There is also fresh corn and chocolate mousse . . . and a very sweet Anjou white wine . . .

N.M.: And burning cheeks to brave the first chill. And what if M. came in here with her red neck wrap and her palest look, her sunniest smile, not looking anything like a conceited *Blancador*?[95]

N.: I always told her: "You won't get me, you little brat!" I will keep saying the same thing, only this time to myself. Anyway, the only women I don't like are the ones that I used to like.

N.M.: I thought that "the strongest friendships are forged in the heat of passion, when there is a sense of the future"?

---

95. *Blancador L'avantageux*, the 1901 novel by Maurice Maindron, recounts the tales of an insufferably arrogant gold digger.

N.: When I said that, I wasn't thinking of M.

N.M.: So even I would have a better chance with you than M. at the moment? T. noticed it as well . . . That's why she is taking me to America.

N.: Throw all that cold water between us?

N.M.: Well, there's always friendship . . .

N.: Friendship is simply love without pleasure!

N.M.: As long as we have bodies and our bodies harmonize with other bodies, shouldn't we seek ecstasy?

N.: Our body is the only part of us that speaks with despotism in the first person.

Waiter: *Mesdames*, do you care for any coffee or liqueur?

N.: A match . . . and the check . . .

N.M.: Look, a last pink candle is falling out of your purse. Should we put it back, or throw it away?

N.: Why do we always need to choose one or the other?

N.M.: You certainly look like you've made up your mind . . .

N.: I am determined to hesitate . . .

N.M.: At least M. and L. are no longer hesitating . . .

N.: How do you know? You never know how much hesitation is hiding behind a decisive action.

N.M.: You are too optimistic. Remember their wire.

N.: That's right, their wire! I was starting to forget about it.

N.M.: When L. was abandoned, did you abandon her? When she learned that you were abandoned, why did she abandon you and run off with the friend that she owed you, even though she denied doing just that?

N.: She was fed that denial by M., who obviously wasn't all that taken with me.

N.M.: But you were taken with her, and L. knew it—she knew it even before anything happened . . . And L. knew very well what M.'s protests were worth. Who hasn't heard them from her?

N.: L. may be able to hold onto her . . . M. needed a master. She was wearing a bracelet from S. that said "I belong to S." when I met her. I was right not to stoke that fire but instead to try and make her a loving friend, an associate.

N.M.: A women that beautiful prefers someone who limits her. Did she at least understand you, and was she grateful?

N.: She is always hoping to be something other than what she is.

N.M.: But you also hoped that she would be something that she is not. Do you know what she called you? "Boule-de-Suif," the "Ford," and who knows what else!

N.: I know . . . I have quite a few names to round out my description: "Beefsteak-and-skinny-fries," "*Extra-dry*," etc., etc. The principled philosopher says it best, noting that youth is nothing but a "tall tale of the aesthete," and my own youth once afforded me prettier names in the past: "April," "*Moon-beam*," "Baby Jesus," "*Honey*," "Israfel"[96] . . .

N.M.: Those names are less nourishing.

N.: And yet my luck over the last six years hasn't been that great.

N.M.: In the twilight of his youth, even Don Juan had to pay his mistresses . . . When your physical capacities are in decline, you are compensated by being at the peak of your other qualities. Someone once said that you were "a woman of her era, a credit to our times."

N.: Times have changed. Who said that about me? A homosexual?

N.M.: Yes, but the two ladies who were with him granted that you are "unique." One of them said: "Her presence brings to mind the music of Debussy."

N.: It's probably the same one who once needed to "hide in order to look at me." Back when the word "déclassé" wasn't yet a compliment, we had a kind of courage to be—what we are.

N.M.: But now, among all these female prisoners with no chains other than cuff links, it is to our credit that we remain as we are.

N. made no comment.

N.M.: So, you are leaving the little pink candle on the table?

N.: It was on a table when we found it: on a birthday cake.

N.M.: And we are celebrating your birthday today, right?[97]

---

96. "The name of an angel in Islam, and the title of a poem by Edgar Allan Poe (1831)." Barney, *Amants féminins*, 142n65.

97. Barney was born on October 31, 1876.

III

Last Dialogue

The Newly Miserable Woman (N.M.): It seems that I never leave your side.

N.: If that were true, you wouldn't notice!

N.M.: They are back in Paris, staying at M.'s. I found out a few minutes ago when I passed by No. 33 to get T.'s photo proofs . . . It seems that they never leave each other . . . They have both moved into M.'s place . . . Did you already know?

N.: Reality is dutifully fulfilling my worst predictions.

N.M.: What plagiarism! Are you all the same disappointed to see what you feared and laid the groundwork for in a moment of Satanic strength, playing out before you?

N.: L. would say angelic.

N.M.: You were the one who dug the hole. They fell in, without even a moment's hesitation.

N.: Done and undone by the ready-made, they made no effort, gave no hint of sudden rebellion.

N.M.: Nevertheless, they are rebelling—against you, the one who succeeded in bringing them together.

N.: What could be more natural? They are united in the interest of the couple. Two against one. Why should I complain? They are no different than—all the others.

N.M.: Did you dare expect anything else? I didn't want to mention it right away, but you have lost weight and you look pale . . .

N.: It's from being in the South—I didn't enjoy being down there all alone.

N.M.: So why did you push them into each other's arms? You didn't count on them staying that way. . . . Are you upset? I think you are, more than you will admit.

N.: We need to suffer a little for our emotions that have gone stale. We owe them that courtesy.

N.M.: So you will safely pine for them here, as a poet, at your writing table.

N.: Regret is a grave robber.

N.M.: Go toward life, toward their life . . . surprise them.

N.: At the same place? No, our entire absence comes between us. Absence: more difficult to violate than a corpse!

N.M.: Use your imagination . . . and take the pressure off the situation. Give it a sense of normalcy.

N.: Dreams are a good stage director, but I am afraid of a rude awakening. Unhappiness breeds unhappiness, and it saps our confidence.

N.M.: With a little bit of madness, we can get through anything . . . Just you wait for the holidays, I can see you coming as a Christmas Tree on Christmas Eve, with a crown of pink candles on your head! A holy martyr with burning candles . . .

N.: That threshold would be harder to cross than a fortified town.

N.M.: Lay siege with your adaptability and strength . . . and your tact . . .

N.: And if they don't have any, I will be at the mercy of a command, a protocol, a pact, an automatic reflex . . . and perhaps the chambermaid has orders.

N.M.: Just admit the spell is broken.

N.: The spell! The spell has chains! My strong desire for M. is beginning to fade.

N.M.: See her again—perhaps that will revive it?

N.: I am not sure if I want to rekindle it. I have often thought about seeing her again. This thought is a shock absorber: I see all that it would not yield.

N.M.: Reality is a useful corrective, perhaps necessary.

N.: And what if L. is there?

N.M.: It would be easy to find a time when she won't be there . . . to hatch a campaign of deception, the moment that L.'s hold over M. weakens sufficiently.

N.: I have no desire for revenge!

N.M.: So, write to them. . . . say you'd like to take them to that park with the camellias . . . in your little house on the Italian Rivera . . .

N.: Too big for two, too small for three . . . I am afraid that we would get bored there! I am afraid that things would get too intimate again too quickly there . . . Women: either they're closed off or wild. They're shameless in letting the truth hang out, just like at a Turkish bath.

N.M.: How do you feel, knowing that they are just around the corner from you? You won't go to No. 33 anymore or even see them?

N.: Resentment. It's obvious that they were meant to be together—and I was meant to be alone.

N.M.: But you must be tempted . . . even just to listen for their footsteps in the courtyard or to glimpse a blue letter on the tray . . .

N.: How did you know?

N.M.: That's the one thing all women know! And don't you find it the least bit surprising that they haven't written to you?

N.: Actually, L. did write me, under the pretext of forwarding an overly effusive letter about me from the writer M.J. She added that she was in Paris for her divorce, and that her stay would be brightened by her memories of our time together . . . and that she was staying more or less in the area at some relative's!

N.M.: So, the divorce case was falsely dismissed—how did you respond?

N.: I didn't! There was no possible response.

N.M.: It's strange, though, that M. hasn't contacted you. Her last letter seemed to suggest that she wants to remember you as a friend.

N.: L. doesn't want to deprive herself of what she has!

N.M.: But at what cost?

N.: At the cost of a new inheritance, if indeed there is one. What does it matter if it is eaten up by M.'s debts, her generosity, or L.'s ulterior motives!

N.M.: In any case, M. is better suited to be L.'s *partner* than yours.

N.: I wouldn't say that. L. wants everything for herself, M. wants everyone else to have everything. They are two different species.

N.M.: For one reason or another, they are always needing money.

N.: M. plays the grand lord, but has no money. She never loves for money, but she loves finding it where she loves. L., on the other hand, calculates everything in advance . . . plans it all out . . .

N.M.: You paint a dark picture.

N.: I call it as I see it!

N.M.: Your conjectures are mean.

N.: Less so than the facts . . . Admit that it has crossed your mind.

N.M.: Everything crosses my mind . . . but not everything should.

N.: Let's try to look clearly at a value that makes so many people lust after someone . . . Money, that vital necessity . . .

N.M.: Trust is just as necessary.

N.: You can't trust L. You forget all too easily that L. is a professional; she got to where she is through material gain.

N.M.: Commerce of the self is still commerce like any other.

N.: As long as you are coarse enough to indulge. And only if you act boldly. L. was the first great courtesan to embellish chivalry with sentimentality—which made it more lucrative. I once remember seeing a letter that she sent to the younger brother of a family. The older brother was her lover—and the father was her appointed keeper:

Young man, you are handsome. I am afraid to love you and suffer. I want to disguise this upsetting feeling under the cloak of materialistic pretense, and so that no one will know that I am in love with you, it will cost you 300 francs per month.

She sent the exact same letter to the older brother with one more zero. She sent the father the same thing with two more zeros.

N.M.: She gave each one the illusion that he was the only one she loved.

N.: Illusion—and then some!

N.M.: That's the unfortunate thing . . . dishonesty . . . because these family secrets never can be kept. Things erupt into drama . . .

N.: But now she can afford to not be interested in money.

N.M.: How so? L. first claims that you are her savior, and that she wants to sacrifice herself too, and then all of a sudden she gets irritated . . . It's simply that she likes getting irritated . . . Her motive is crystal clear.

N.: Crystal is not always clear. When you examine this stone, you can see how the light and dark sections are often mixed together—we no longer can tell where one ends and the other begins.

N.M.: If you yourself don't need to, you are not suspicious enough, so let's leave this public woman to public opinion; they deserve each other.

N.: That's where you are wrong—public opinion is not devoid of subtlety, but it's quick to judge. It doesn't like when a person flaunts one thing and does another. L. made herself out to be a victim of an assassination, and she shouldn't resuscitate herself too quickly.

N.M.: See, you agree with me . . . If L. acts otherwise, she has good reasons of her own.

N.: People don't become more honest, but they do get better at hiding what they're not! It is true that M. would be more than willing to hand over her inheritance to L., to give her everything that she has. Didn't she beg me to force her to get legal counsel? "Otherwise," she told me, "once I have my fortune at my disposal, I will squander it on my current mistress. If it were D.S., I would buy her a cabaret, if it were the duchess of A., a tiara. Money is of no importance to me." But what will prevent her from making the same argument to L.: Since you are so organized, don't let me waste my money every which way, keep it . . . take charge . . . since we will always be together!"

N.M.: That's just it, and then L. will look like she is doing it for M.'s good, to protect her, since she is M.'s keeper.

N.: Impossible!

N.M.: Because she won't keep M., but she will certainly keep her money.[98]

_____

98. The manuscript in the Bibliothèque Littéraire Jacques Doucet does not indicate which speaker says what. Because of this ambiguity, it is a challenge to

N.: If these predictions should prove you wrong, I would be thrilled . . . for both of them.

N.M.: What magnanimity! But I fear that I'm not wrong. Lovers come and go, but numbers never do. And L. knows it better than anyone. And if her goals in war are purely sentimental, why lie to you, why exclude you to this point? . . . She is more afraid of you on a financial level than a sentimental level. . . . if I dare say so . . .

N.: That's less flattering! In the beginning, M. blamed me for introducing her to L.

N.M.: She'll blame you all the more in the end.

N.: She complained about how hard it had been to leave S.G. and that it would be even harder to leave L.

N.M.: That's what people should think about when they start a love affair!

N.: She added that we were mere children compared to L. Other times L. was a lamb trembling as the predator approached. Trying to find a happy medium, M. goes from one extreme to the other . . . she is so taken by quantity, she cannot see quality. Don't forget to what extent her laugh and her singing lack quality. It was just like her to say of my big hands: "Your pretty little hands." Her lack of discernment goes as far as declaring each one of these women "my pearly lady of the lake."

N.M.: For once it's relevant.

N.: As a matter of fact, L.'s iridescent face seems to be made of the living mother of pearl she has received from the men that she has solicited so often in her trade.

N.M.: Regardless of what motive is behind her present shenanigans, make this a pretext and ban her from your home forever.[99] There will never be a better time.

---

decipher. The French edition is inaccurate in this section (Barney, *Amants féminins*, 148) and it has been corrected here.

99. Although Barney did not know it at the time, the affair between de Pougy, Barney, and Franchetti did wind up destroying the twenty-eight-year friendship between de Pougy and Barney. Rapazzini, *Elisabeth de Gramont*, 392.

N.: I'm not looking for one! And it would be cowardly to do it now that her husband has left. She even told me that, because of that, she would be coming to all my receptions from now on![100]

N.M.: All your friends suffer because you were weak enough to impose her presence on them.

N.: Weak—you should say strong.

N.M.: How many of your friends no longer wanted to visit you for fear of seeing her? Everywhere she goes, she undermines the atmosphere and leaves her mark.

N.: A beauty mark.

N.M.: So be it, but witty banter demands both more—and less.

N.: Well, she certainly doesn't make herself scarce.

N.M.: Make her scarce from your heart and memory, and, if necessary, from your salon. What has she ever done to you that wasn't either selfish or tactless—in exchange for so many years of concern and devotion?

N.: She's the one who is staying away—not me . . . Maybe it will turn out that they are simply pretending to be exclusive with each other.

N.M.: In any case, their game is lacking in honesty and sensitivity.

N.: If they aren't following the rules of the game, perhaps cheating excites them more.

N.M.: You have the same philosophy as your friend, Lady W. When someone indebted to her is inconsiderate, she seems thrilled. She took pleasure in confirming that the person indebted "was none other than what he was." One time I wanted to tell her about a betrayal, indignant that someone could go to such lengths to be deceitful. I exclaimed: "It is dishonest to take advantage of you like that." "Forget it!" she responded. "You really don't want the tables to be turned!" Instead of killing them with kindness, you should remember your own line:

Brand her, but do it as a master.

---

100. Barney settled in Paris at the turn of the century, where she began a literary salon in 1909 that drew leading European and Anglo-American writers and intellectuals to her home every Friday. She published *Aventures de l'esprit* in 1929 as a tribute to her salon and to her many friendships cultivated there.

N.: Yes, clearly M. wasn't mature enough for this kind of association.

N.M.: Do you have any doubt? Don't make yourself out to be better than you are: tender, deceived, melting. Reveal your diabolical side, throw out your demons: they are suffocating you. Love as you write: with cynicism, with science. Why hide behind this faint and feigned docility that is your—mask . . . Since living is your art, dear Lucifer, at least have the decency to live according to your own style. Why are you worrying without anything to show for it? Write down this story and dedicate it . . . to M.'s mistresses, for example. They will take comfort in it.

N.: They have a better comfort: forgetting!

N.M.: M. deserves capital punishment, in any case.

N.: L. certainly does, but I would be carrying out my own death sentence in executing them.

N.M.: I wouldn't worry about that, because no one plays a starring role when we expose our truth. Our stardom is made up of everything we conceal! For once you can write down the truth without being indiscreet, and this saga gives you material for a short novel. Yes, since everything didn't go into the fire, nothing is preventing you: neither true love, nor a heart too big. You can make quite a humorous book out of this. Would you like me to help you?

N.: Why are you so openly my ally . . . and more Catholic than the Pope?

N.M.: Because the Pope isn't Catholic enough![101]

N.: Why is it that after seeking others, neither of us is complete? Others—always others—what do they bring us?

N.M.: We should be happy if they don't belittle us to their advantage.

N.: Perhaps . . . but why bother stopping them? In thinking about my life, all my lives evolved through experiences that are more or less the same. The best and the worst of them are pulled by some vibration, gravitate for a time, and then fall away together.

---

101. The translation changes the original metaphor, which was based on being "more royal than the king."

N.M.: You so like to see yourself alone—one against the rest! After all, why would it bother you being unique—or being the third one?

N.: In my entire human experience, only one woman was like me: isolated, resistant to this earthly law—radiating her warmth and clarity from her own center . . .

You alone appeared to me as what people ever seek . . .[102]

N.M.: But then why keep searching after you found her?

N.: Because we undergo eclipses.

N.M.: Admit that you overdo it!

N.: In periods of darkness, we still cry together; that is all that seems left of our love—while we wait.

N.M.: For what?

N.: We take turns holding the torch made of out of both of our essences. Soon or in the next revolution of the cycle, it will be her turn to prove to me the quality of her fire. She won't let me down, and I won't let her down. And one day, everything will be consumed.

N.M.: But your incandescent ideal exists! Why do you play recklessly with fire? I told you that M. would burn you.

N.: The worst isn't that we burn ourselves, but that the fire goes out.

END

(but there is no end . . .)

NATALIE CLIFFORD BARNEY[103]

102. "Alfred de Vigny, Éloa, ou, La soeur des anges, III." Barney, *Amants féminins*, 151n67. The English text is from Alfred de Vigny, *Eloa, or the Sister of the Angels*, trans. Alan Corré (n.p., 2012).

103. "For the second time, Barney affixes her handwritten signature to the end of the typescript." Barney, *Amants féminins*, 152n68.

NATALIE CLIFFORD BARNEY (1876–1972) was an American-born writer of poems, epigrams, and memoirs. She was also well known for her weekly salon in Paris that drew avant-garde writers, artists, musicians, and intellectuals to her home for more than sixty years.

CHELSEA RAY is an associate professor of French and comparative literature at the University of Maine at Augusta. She has been honored as a Chevalier des palmes académiques by France's Ministry of Education.